FINDING FEALTY

June Russell Laing

June Russell Publishing

Copyright © 2020 June Russell Laing

All rights reserved

The characters and events portrayed in this book are fictitious. Any similarity to real persons, living or dead, is coincidental and not intended by the author.

No part of this book may be reproduced, or stored in a retrieval system, or transmitted in any form or by any means, electronic, mechanical, photocopying, recording, or otherwise, without express written permission of the publisher.

ISBN 9798559215983

Cover design by: Art Painter
Library of Congress Control Number: 2018675309
Printed in the United States of America

ACKNOWLEDGEMENT

I would like to thank my husband Andrew Laing for his editing assistance, encouragement, unwavering support, unlimited patience and ability to rescue me from technology disasters. Andrew – you're a star!

"I am alone in the midst of these happy, reasonable voices. All these creatures spend their time explaining, realising happily that they agree with each other. In Heaven's name, why is it so important to think the same things all together."

JEAN-PAUL SARTRE, NAUSEA

CONTENTS

Title Page	1
Copyright	2
Dedication	3
Epigraph	4
Preface	7
CHAPTER 1 - PRODDY DOGS AND FEEN-YINS	9
CHAPTER 2 - HAPPINESS IS	24
CHAPTER 3 - JESUS SAVES	36
CHAPTER 4 - SEX AND DRUGS AND ROLL-YOUR-OWNS	46
CHAPTER 5 - MAZEL TOV	55
CHAPTER 6 - LEGS LIKE PELE	64
CHAPTER 7 - CORNUCOPIA	75
CHAPTER 8 - MANY PATHS UP THE SAME MOUNTAIN	82
CHAPTER 9 - YOU CAN CHOOSE YOUR FRIENDS	94
CHAPTER 10 - THE MONSTER IN THE CUPBOARD	102
CHAPTER 11 - FOR WHOM THE BELLS	108
CHAPTER 12 - COMING HOME	123
CHAPTER 13 - TROUBLE AT T'MILL	129
EPILOGUE	138
About The Author	143
Book Club Discussion Questions	145

PREFACE

A young girl born to a deprived 1960's Glasgow council estate sets off to find meaning and belonging beyond her birthright. Through entertaining anecdote and misadventure, she explores the deeper philosophical questions of religion and tribalism, the sacrifices that must be made to belong and ultimately to whom we owe fealty.

CHAPTER 1 - PRODDY DOGS AND FEEN-YINS

"Are ye a Feen-yin or a Proddy Dog?"
"**Are** ye a Feen-yin or a Proddy Dog?"
The year was 1966, the place a greasy street on a run-down Glasgow council estate. To judge by his rapt expression, the answer was critical to this congested, ferret-faced boy.

"Well? Whit **are** ye?"

I hesitated. For I neither understood the question, nor knew the answer.

Rolling his eyes at his open-mouthed pals, ferret-face sighed and tossed me a life ring:

"Whit **school** dae ye go tae?"

Ah. Now this I did know.

"Craigie Park."

"A Proddy Dog then."

This was clearly the right answer. Satisfied, the boys leapt onto their Choppers and sped off into the deeper recesses of the estate.

I didn't know what I was. I only knew what I wasn't, since no-one had thought to mention what I was. I wasn't Feen-yin, I knew that much for sure. I'd been told we hated Catholics. Why? No-one had thought to mention that either.

I suppose I might have worked out that I was Protestant had I known that Proddy was the opposite of Feen-yin. But you can only work with what you've been given.

So here I was, just seven years old, confronted with the knotty concept of religious affiliation. Except it wasn't. This was my introduction to tribal affiliation. A quite different thing altogether.

◆ ◆ ◆

On reflection, I might have noticed that there were no Feen-yins at the Lodge.

At 6 p.m. on a Saturday, my brothers and I were decked out in cheap, scratchy tartan – me in a blocky, shapeless frock with a crude elasticated waist and my brothers in badly cut, ill-fitting waistcoats. Excited, we skipped along the oily streets to what was, in all honesty, a rather depressing scout hut of a building with a permanently sticky floor.

Oh how we loved the Lodge. Even Mam seemed to like it. We loved spinning one another round and lobbing each other under the tables, breathless and sniggering as we stomped and pranced to an accordion, a fiddle, two tin whistles and a great booming drum. When the sweaty-faced adults weren't looking, we drained the scant dregs of their drinks and burped in each other's faces.

And – yes – I know what you're thinking. Young innocents shouldn't be indoctrinated into the hate and vitriol that is the Orange Lodge. And you'd be right in a way. But, genuinely, we had no idea why we were there. I don't recall being subjected to any particular hate-speak, just jolly staggering drunks and other giggling, half-tiddly kids.

I don't doubt that you, the public, know more about the Lodge than we kids did - the bigotry, the provocative sectarianism, the never ending re-visiting of the dark historic battles between Protestant and Catholic. Add to that the violence, the street abuse, the secrecy, the elaborate ceremonies and archaic titles and, yes, it's a toxic cocktail.

You know and I know now that it's scarcely religious at all. If it had once had a more spiritual foundation, that had long since eroded. What we were dealing with was tribal, political and unforgiving. And while my parents, did, it seems, subscribe to this repulsive apartheid, they did not, at least in the early years, appear to impart that particular ugliness to their offspring. As a youngster, being Proddy – even if you didn't know what you were, **especially** if you didn't know what you were – seemed like reasonably good fun.

But, you say, not letting me off the hook quite that easily - surely you sang the songs?

Yes, I suppose we did. But what does *'The Famine's Over, Why Don't You Go Home?'* mean to a small child? Not a lot, I'm sure you'd agree.

Oh and we never went on the marches. Just so you know.

Alas, despite the archaic nature of the roles and language, the dark long-ago-ness of the original feud, the Orange tribe marched on. And it marches still, the hate enthusiastically revisited, renewed and regurgitated.

For better or worse, we were steeped in it. In every word and deed, subtle and not so subtle, those we looked to for guidance transmitted it. And so, inevitably, we knew of no other way to be.

Of course I was aware that there were people much better off than we were. The adults talked of little else. But I was also quite certain that there were people much worse off. I imagined, therefore, that we'd be somewhere slap-bang in the middle.

With hindsight, my assessment of our socio-economic ranking was uncomfortably wide of the mark. But how was I to know? I didn't **feel** deprived. I didn't yet know what 'not deprived' would look like. The only information I had was what my tribe presented to me.

For all the hatred and the conjured-up social divisions, the one thing that united Proddies and Feen-yins was a visceral suspicion of and loathing for establishment in any form – corporation, government, school inspectors, social workers, police and the legions of 'do-gooders' who came and went in waves.

'They' – all of them - were against us in every conceivable way. Everyone knew that. The government spied on us, vetoed any attempt to improve our lot and withheld monies that were rightfully ours.

Whatever 'the government' did put in place, ostensibly for our betterment – community centre, museum, schools, library and leisure centre – they were not rewarded with a level of gratitude that might reasonably have been expected.

Not at all. The monies spent could and should have been spent better. On what, I never understood, for no-one seemed to think it necessary to say what they actually wanted. Only what they did not.

Church was different. Whichever church we were affiliated to was **on our side**. And no-one else's of course. We gave them a share of what little money we had and they gave us what we needed most in the world. False promises and an identity in return for fealty. They set the rules, we followed the rules. For without them, who could we possibly be?

I would share with you my own opinion – that whatever necessities our community failed to provide for itself, the council, the government or some charity provided. We did okay. And that's the truth.

We had just three TV channels in those early days. Only one channel put on cartoons on the weekend and for a measly half hour at that. All remaining screen time seemed given over to endless, interminably boring boxing, wrestling and Match of the Day. If we stayed home we were endlessly shushed by Da or by Mam on Da's behalf.

So, at sparrow's fart on Saturday mornings, my brother Roddy and I would throw back the covers, toss some Rice Crispies and milk into bowls and park ourselves in the living room just in time for Looney Tunes. We'd rinse our bowls out in the sink then race one another to the library on the main street, arms outstretched, screeching the Loony Tunes theme tune with gathering speed and rising pitch.

I might have used the term 'bookish' for Roddy and I if I weren't wary of the assumptions you might make. Truth is, we were ordinary, scuffed and snottery estate kids who loved to play out, wreak fairly harmless havoc and generally have fun.

But we did love books. All types of books, any books. There was nothing we wouldn't read. Each morning at breakfast, we'd pause, spoons in mid-air, while we scanned the same front, back and sides of the cereal boxes.

Penelope - Pippy - the giggly, moon-faced library assistant, joked that she couldn't keep up with us.

"**You** pair would read the phone book!!"

Pippy chewed the ends of a never-ending stream of pencils which said 'Penelope' in gold letters on the side. She giggled and rolled her eyes as she pointed out the lettering:

"When I was your age, my mother started buying boxes of these for me. I couldn't understand why I had pencils with penny lopey on them."

I told Roddy I wanted pencils with Deb-orah on them.

Roddy and Pippy blinked. Then burst into peals of laughter.

Pippy would sneak new stock under the counter for us and put in transfer requests for anything she didn't have but thought we would enjoy. Our library tickets entitled us to just four books at a time, but Pippy made up an extra card for our older brother David. Or Davey he liked to be called. Davey didn't read, so we made the most of his allocation.

Roddy was eighteen months younger than me and by the time I was nine and he seven, we'd both read the entire series of H.E. Todd's Bobby Brewster; all twenty two of Enid Blyton's Famous Five books; Alan Garner's The Weirdstone of Brising Amen, The Owl Service, The Moon of Gomrath and Elidor; Kastner's Emile and the Detectives; Clive King's Stig of the Dump; Serraillier's The Silver Sword; the first three of Joan Aiken's Wolves of Willoughby Chase series; and anything by Roald Dahl that had been written by then – The Gremlins, Charlie and the Chocolate Factory, James and the Giant Peach and Fantastic Mr. Fox.

Pippy took huge personal pride in getting the 'best of the best' books for us, so when a grubby, dog-eared copy of Louisa May Allcott's 'Little Women' found its way into our house via a box of toys from a jumble sale, I waved it in front of her.

"**Penny Lopeeee**! You missed this!"

She chuckled affectionately.

"Oooh....**of course**! I thought it might be too old or maybe a bit slow for you, but you're a couple of right wee book gobblers!"

She ruffled my hair and tweaked Roddy's nose.

I for one was hooked from Alcott's first sentence:

"Christmas won't be Christmas without any presents."

My best friend Mhairead and I took turns being the March girls. She inevitably chose to be Beth and played out an exaggerated deathbed scene over and over with increasing melodrama. I was always Jo.

Like the museum and the library, school was an enchanted portal. A gateway to a vast and wondrous universe, books and art were magic carpets, transporting us to unimaginable places, entire new visions, alternative worlds with exotic back stories. We couldn't get enough.

When I wasn't reading, I loved to write. When I'd galloped through the homework pieces we wrote for school, I loved to sketch out little children's stories and made clumsy first attempts at poetry. My teacher, Miss Campbell gave me a spare school jotter which I used as a kind of diary and each night before sleeping I would jot down thoughts, feelings and ideas for stories and poems.

Inevitably the diary's hiding place was discovered. Which might not have been quite so bad if it hadn't been discovered by the worst possible person - my brother Davey.

My best friend Mhairead was that rare, unspeakable abomination – the offspring of the union between a Feen-yin and a Proddy Dog. Mhairead's Irish mother Bridie was the Feen-yin and Mhairead's dad Bill was the minister of our one and only Protestant church – a ruggedly handsome, 'hale fellow well met' kind of guy. Mam hugely disapproved of the union.

"Deborah" she said, rolling her eyes "It's like a dog mating with a cat, is it not?"

There was much speculation as to why any union involving a Proddy and a Feen-yin could happen, let alone sire just the one child. The local gossips were unanimous in their condemnation - Bridie had turned away from Bill, reneged on her marital undertakings and lost herself in contemplation of the world beyond.

Once, Mhairead confided in a low whisper "my mother thinks Jesus is her boyfriend".

And if the rapturous gaze Bridie bestowed upon her garish representations of the Sacred Heart were to count as evidence, there did seem to be a certain lovesick element to her devotions. This Jesus, of course, was a decidedly non-Semitic, fantasy Jesus with pale, translucent skin and impossibly blue eyes. An airbrushed, Mills and Boon Jesus.

There were many rumours that Bill was 'putting it about'. A full four years before the Thorn Birds' raunchy prose warmed the upper thighs of the world's middle-class women, the estate wifeys hung on Bill's every utterance and contrived whatever excuses they could to bask in his hallowed presence.

The excuses often took the form of gifts for the apple of Bill's eye – his precious pearl, his unsullied princess Mhairead. They knitted shapeless cardi's with little leather-look buttons; mittens tied together with knitted cords; hats with gigantic pom-poms and – when the fashion presented itself – chunky little Mexican ponchos with, of all things, matching French berets.

They baked anaemic looking shortbread, over-jammed empire biscuits and knobbly brown objects which looked like dog turds.

Mamie Clark who could neither knit nor bake, was waaaay more imaginative. She presented Bill with a foul-mouthed, 'possessed' budgie that – naturally "required an exorcism".

These women were, of course, hardly the well-heeled, pearl twisting ladies of the Women's Institute. They were, by and large, what were unkindly referred to in Glaswegian parlance as 'Hairy

Marys', 'Bauchles' or 'Wee Fat Coats'.

Eager consumers of bargain basement Woman's Weekly romance fiction, these rotund, world-weary, love-starved women were proffered a glimpse of Paradise by the-hero-known-as-Bill. But not the glimpse he was supposed to offer.

Bill – it was reported – had bragged to his brother-in-law:

"They treat me like a god round here Sean. They might not be bonny, but these women know how to make a man feel wanted."

Mhairead and her family were not born to the estate and so were noticeably different to us locals. Mhairead was soft spoken and had exaggerated good manners. She was what we called 'perjink'. The house she lived in she referred to as 'The Man's'. I often wondered why the man didn't want the house for himself given that it was – if not exactly grand – a lot better than what were used to living in.

When the perennial requirements for school uniforms or new clothes came around, most of what we needed was facilitated by something called 'The Provident Cheque'. Only a small number of shops actually took 'The Provi'. Mam's emporium of choice was a down-at-heel establishment called Kumar's, which was run by four Mohammeds and an Omar.

Mhairead's family – on the other hand – satisfied their sartorial requirements from something called the Littlewoods Catalogue. I looked on in envy as Mhairead was first to acquire that year's must have items. She was first to sport T-bar platforms, a poncho, oxford bags and a fitted blazer with a dark border round the edges. I think perhaps it was called a sailor's jacket? I wasn't aware then that The Provi and The Catalogue were forms of 'tick' and that Mhairead's family were substantially in debt.

Mhairead had acquired – no doubt from 'the Catalogue'- a rose-sprigged, doll's tea set made of real porcelain. She would set it out on a picnic blanket in the communal gardens for a formal doll's tea party. I say 'gardens'. In reality it was a bare patch of what used to be grass surrounded by a bent and rusty iron fence. Where there had been grass there was now a huge patch of scorched earth where the euphemistically described 'communal bonfires' took place. In reality, it was the spot where the local yobs, inevitably led by my brother Davey, honed their arson skills. Due to a fad for lobbing empty aerosol cans into the flames, many of said yobs were missing the front sections of their hair and had no eyebrows or eyelashes.

Mhairead and I would set out her blanket amidst the weeds, greasy puddles, cigarette butts, broken bottles and empty crisp bags. My doll Bonny bore the scars of an earlier encounter with Davey. Her hair had been set on fire, her eyes were poked through and she had multiple felt marker 'spots'. But she still felt up for a social gathering and a cup of invisible tea. Bonny was a trooper.

While slurping our 'tea' we would play-act the gossip we routinely heard around the older women, surreptitiously lowering our voices and looking round for witnesses at the appropriate moments:

"I heard Margaret Brady's got *the big C.*"

"Mamie Reilly's man says she's *goin' through the change* and bein' a right bitch."

"Sandra Forrest's had her wean now *and her man says it's goat the minister's face.*"

My granny would always caution Mam:

"*Wee dugs hae lang lugs.*"

Well, as little dogs with long ears we may well have heard what we shouldn't have. Mercifully, we did not understand.

And speaking of not understanding, for most of my childhood years my mother referred to me, through the most pursed of lips, as "Mrs. Simpson". I didn't know what it meant, but her tone suggested it was no compliment.

Unfailingly presiding over our tea parties was 'Auld Watchie' – a sad-faced, crumpled old crone whose pale apparition hovered at the window all day every day. The local wags had helpfully spray painted 'Auld Watchie' on the wall next to her window, with an arrow pointing to the precise spot.

I often wondered what Auld Watchie's story was. There were rumours that she'd been part of a gypsy family of horse traders and that she'd had a pet goat. The council – so the story went –

had 'forced' them into a council house which had caught fire in the night, killing the entire family with the exception of Watchie herself. And there she sat, day after day, with apparently nothing to do but watch life play out beneath her window.

Shuggy Lomas's dad said he'd when he was young he'd seen her pushing an old pram around the estate, collecting firewood, plant cuttings and old shoes.

She was a fixture in our lives. A navigable compass point. So much so that, when one day she was no longer there and a new family moved into her flat, we were all at sea. Strange that she who was never 'of-us' when alive, graduated to 'missing from us' by the act of dying. And upon the new family was thrust the mantel of 'not of us'. Tribal allegiance is a fickle thing.

You'd think with Mhairid being a 'mongrel' or a 'Heinz 57' with a name that sounded like 'My Rat' she'd be prime fodder for bullies. But – for reasons I didn't then understand – the bullies closed ranks and protected her.

As her best friend, it appeared I'd acquired the same immunity. Which was somewhat fortunate, since it allowed me to enunciate my words clearly like Mhairead did. In general, estate kids who affected to speak 'proper' were accused of being 'right up their own arse' and generally received a sound boot up said arse.

Mhairead's mother Bridie appeared to have negotiated some kind of compromise with Bill. While Mhairead could go to the Protestant school, she would attend Mass three times a week with her mother. For her soul belonged to Jesus and Jesus wasn't for the Proddies. We had somebody else - some vague and shadowy presence referred to as the Son of God.

One day Mhairead took me upstairs to her pink-swagged bedroom and showed me her communion dress. It was a short, white, heavily ruffled number, a miniature version of the prevailing bubble-bath fashion in a wedding dress. It was completed with a stiff little veil with wired edges, white bow-fronted shoes and tiny lace gloves for the baby bride.

"You goin' to be Jesus's girlfriend too?" I ventured.

Mhairead looked affronted and answered in her mother's voice: "Jesus won't **loike** you for saying that."

I grimaced. "Sorry pal. So what's it all about then?"

Instantly recovered, she explained in hushed, reverent tones:

"We're given the wafer. It's the ac-tual body of Christ. And later – when we're older - we'll get the wine. And that's the ac-tual blood of Christ. It's called trans-submagination."

I didn't get it. Of course I didn't. And I'm pret-ty sure Mhairead didn't get it either.

I thought about how different the Catholic God was to ours. He liked gaudy pantomime hats and outfits; biddable flocks of little boys in nightdresses, smoky handbags and baby brides.

Whereas our God liked....well actually I wasn't sure what He liked. I asked my brother Roddy.

"Rodders...what does our God like? I mean what is it He wants us to do?"

He looked up from his book and grinned.

"What **ho**, young Deborah. Lashings of ginger beer, what?"

"Aww....stop it. I'm being serious Roddy."

"Hmm. I dunno what He would want. Not very much. I think we just have to not like Feen-yins."

I did genuinely think that Protestants and Catholics worshipped – or at the very least, derived their identity from – different Gods. Well, given the evidence, you would, wouldn't you?

Now, if I've given you the impression that my own parents had neglected my religious instruction, then I'm hugely at fault. Without fail, for two hours every Sunday, Roddy and I were marched off to Sunday School. So kind of the church to offer free babysitting. Davey, being Davey, refused to go.

Having visited many ethereal and spiritually inspiring churches in my later years, I have to confess that, by comparison, our local church was an apologetic, dingy affair. Built of a bland, yellowish brick in the 1950's, it lacked any ornamentation other than one arched window above the scuffed platform that served as the altar.

Where fresh and fragrant flowers might have lifted our spirits, faded plastic tulips collected dead flies and dust. The occasional shaft of sunlight illuminated the baked-on grime on the curved window, that being the sole, sad intimation of the sacred and the world beyond.

Bill – in his element - would strut and grandstand, quoting parables, random lines of scripture and supposedly illuminating stories which we either didn't understand or didn't care to understand. Mostly we just waited patiently for the bit where they got out the drawing paper and crayons and the one solitary penny chew.

If there **had** been a place where someone might mention that we were - if only technically - Protestant, this would surely have been the one. Alas, I swear to you, it did not happen.

I do remember one Sunday when Bill was relating his favourite parable – that of the Prodigal Son – Roddy dug me in the ribs and whispered:

"If the Prodigal son had come home a Catholic, would there have been rejoicing in Heaven? I. Think. **Not**."

We giggled into our clean white hankies and pretended to have coughing fits. For whatever twattery you engaged in outside, you did not laugh in church.

Although nowhere near as bad as being a Feen-yin, being a 'teacher's pet' was a hugely undesirable state of being. I happened into this entirely by accident. It was Miss Campbell who personally took on the role of delivering me from the deep vale of ignorance that was our estate. She looked like Princess Anne on the outside – that is, all parched and prim. But between you and me, she was all melting moments on the inside. The other kids called her 'Auld Maid' or 'Stinky Cat Lady'. As it happens, she neither stank nor ever mentioned any fondness for felines.

Miss Campbell took me under her wing, keeping me after school for extra lessons. Like Mam, she always called me 'Deborah' rather than Debbie or Debs. But her tone was fond at least.

I feel guilty when I think of Miss Campbell. For it seems she misinterpreted my insatiable curiosity and willingness to listen for a thirst for knowledge. Alas, my hunger was not for knowledge per se, but some manner of certainty, something I could hang my little bobble hat on.

Miss Campbell strove to open the world up to me, to show me what was out there, everything I could bring to my life simply through the power of education. Alas, my ambitions were somewhat lesser. I craved being a part of something meaningful. I wanted to have something concrete to believe. I wanted to belong.

So what – you may well ask - was my problem? I was **born** to belong. Belonging-ness in the fullest sense of the word was a given. It was clearly laid out on a very large plate. Our tribe had a very detailed and specific web of structures, norms, expectations, codes and even – for gawdsakes – a prescribed football team to support.

You knew what side you were on, what you had to do and you knew what you should not. No need to figure any of it out for yourself. Indeed, you were strongly encouraged not to go figuring anything out for yourself.

But, for whatever reason, my tribe did not have my heart.

And what of the Feen-yins? Pretty much the same I guess. The actual expectations and codes would be different, of course, but the all-inclusive embrace, the leaving-nothing-to-chance-ness was the same.

Our names for the Catholics ran the whole gamut:

Fenian; Papist; Mick; Taig; Sponger; Bead Rattler; Bog Trotter; Tim; Paddy; Tattie Muncher; Soap Dodger . . .

And they responded with their own insults:

Orangie; Jaffa; Proddy; Proddy Dog; Blue Nose; Drum Basher; Current Bun (Hun); Billy Boy and – of course – Soap Dodger.

Well, at least we had something in common.

When we'd worked our way through all of the sectarian insults, we fell back on some more generic ones:

"Yer brother's a bawbag."

"Yer da sells Avon."

"Yer sister's goat an erse like a bag o' washin."

"Yer granpa's a jakey."

"Yer maw's goat balls n' yer da loves it."

"If your brains were cotton wool, ye widnae huv enough for a mouse's tampax."

"Yer maw looks like two pun o' mince in a one pun bag."

"Yer maw steals snowmens' noses fur her lentil soup."

Our warring worlds would collide from time to time – most noticeably as we were transported to our separate schools on our separate buses. The Feen-yins wore the green uniforms of St. Cuthbert's, the Proddies the brown of Craigie Park.

When our respective buses drew up alongside one another we whooped, hollered and cat-called like caged animals, the lads pressing their bare arses up against the bus windows. The drivers had long since given up trying to assert control.

There was a song our boys loved to sing. I think it went:

"Ian, Ian can ye see 'im?

Lifting his frock for Father Liam."

And I could. See 'im' I mean. Curtseying to the priest n'all. No wonder they called him out.

The Feen-yins had songs for us too, of course. But they were by and large rather unimaginative and centred around the unfortunate turd-like colour of our uniforms.

And we had this ritual if one of us inadvertently got too close to the enemy. We'd shout:

"Vaccinated, five ten!" as we jumped backwards and…..get this for irony, we would **make the sign of the cross.**

Dear god, you couldn't write this stuff.

And the enemy would do the same – though to be fair they were much slicker with the genuflecting, having had much more practice than us.

So there you had this crazy, ritual dance of two polarised communities leaping backwards from one another, crossing themselves and affecting to look thoroughly disgusted.

Eat your heart out Margaret Mead. Forget far away Samoa, there was enough social and cultural anthro-**bloody**-pology on our estate. Could have kept you going for years.

I often wondered how it was that communities who lived cheek by jowl could turn out so differently. Maybe Mam was right about the cats and dogs. But then again, I had no idea of the history. None of us understood it or cared to understand it.

It was just what we did; what we were expected to do. As our forebears had done and what it was expected we would condition our own broods to do. The behaviours were adhered to when the rationales – such as they ever were - were long since forgotten.

CHAPTER 2 - HAPPINESS IS . . . .

The highlight of most days – other than exceptional events such as Christmas, Easter and any time Rangers beat Celtic – was queuing up for the penny tray. Mrs. Barr, the caretaker's wife, had converted a small, lock up garage adjacent to our school into a magical sweet shop. If the roller shutter was up, the trays were out.

We each had just one penny to spend, but oh what riches one penny could buy. On the tray were tiny twisted packets of love hearts and parma violets; flying saucers which were saucer-shaped packages of pink and yellow rice paper filled with sherbet; two-for-a-penny fruit salad chews and black jacks which turned our teeth and tongues black; cola bottles; bazooka joes; white chocolate mice; chiclets; wax lips; and swizzle lollies.

Mrs. Barr tried to be patient as each child fondled the riches one by precious one with fingers that had been up noses or down the front of trousers. But inevitably she would lose it and shout:

"Right you lot. I huvnae **goat** a' day!"

On our estate, most mothers – including Mam - had factory jobs, cleaning jobs or both. That being the case, it fell to the older kids to keep the households functioning.

Girls as young as six made up baby bottles from the big government-issued blue and white tins of National Dried Milk. I remember a girl in my class confessing to having added, at various times, a dollop of jam, a spoonful of custard powder and some powdered

Chivers jelly granules to her youngest brother's bottle:

"Poor wean hus the same bottle of milk every bloomin' day. Must be right borin."

Some of the estate girls got pregnant so young that they'd be making bottles simultaneously for their Mam's babies and their own. These were Proddy girls of course. Young unmarried Feenyin girls did not get pregnant. Or so it was said, though some girls did mysteriously disappear only to reappear some time later.

Uncomplaining, estate kids would scrape shit off their siblings' nappies and boil the bejeezus out of them in the ubiquitous Burco boiler. They'd clean the house and re-clean it the next day.

They knew the cost of bread and milk and they knew the shame of carrying 'the note' on a Thursday to neighbours to ask for the loan of a pound to buy enough bread and milk until the pay-packet came the following day, or asking *sotto voce* whether the food we'd just bought could be added to our family's growing tick book at the local corner shop. Debt was frowned upon of course, but our local retailers operated on the tacit understanding of discretion in return for payment in the fullness of time.

Our Burco boiler had more than one use. When it wasn't bubbling in excrement, it was the vessel of choice for my granny to immerse the flour, suet and spice filled, tied linen bag in which she steamed her annual Christmas clootie dumpling.

For twenty four hours the zesty waft of dried fruit, nutmeg and cinnamon would infuse our home, making our tummies rumble and our hearts soar with the anticipation of Christmas magic.

And I'm pretty sure the bag was always pretty well sealed.

Households on our estate were divided into respectable and non-respectable. 'Respectable' households were judged primarily on two counts – the state of their front windows and the arrangement of clothes on the washing line.

Front windows were shone to perfection and curtains swagged

and arranged in perfect symmetry. Woe betide the child who opened the curtains and left them –'hauf hung' or 'lop-sided'. Every front facing window had a centrepiece – a vase of plastic flowers or perhaps a nice piece of Lladro or Capodimonte. Not the real thing of course. The clumsy-seamed, mass produced versions that could be bought at All Kinds of Everything under the stinky bridge on Argyle Street.

Hanging out the washing was an art and any failure to follow the rules was met with extreme social disapproval. You could only put washing out on your own specified day. If it rained on your day, too bad. And you had to use your own washing line and washing pole and take them back in when you were done.

Nappies –however well used – had to be white, white, white. They were scrubbed and boiled till the fabric grew thin and holes appeared. Holes were fine. Stains a no-no.

All underpants had to be hung together with a discernible space of at least half an inch between each. Boys pants together; girls pants together. Socks were hung altogether in matching pairs and with the ankle portion uppermost. Sheets and towels were looped over the washing line with the edges precisely matching up. A particular challenge for the smaller kids who had to jump to get bigger items over the line.

And it if rained – dear **God** if it rained – you had to bring the whole lot back in, wait till the rain stopped and put it all back out again.

You **could** drape the whole sweaty, dripping load over the kitchen pulley. It took more than one kid to haul up the ropes and if you let it go or if the rope snapped you had to hope your kitchen floor was clean.

Inside-drying washing could be hung any way you liked, but it tended to make the windows steam up. And **that** was a no-no.

Laundering was a complicated business.

In the summer holidays when the adults were out at work and the chores were done, we kids had the run of the estate. Our fertile imaginations and energy levels were easily up to the task of finding ways to pass the long swathes of time from early breakfast till dinner.

There were so many games I can scarcely remember the full list. Central to all of them, however, was strict sectarian separation. We did not play with 'dirty' Feen-yins.

We played Peever, our version of Hopscotch; skipping ropes (incorporating Double Dutch); Chinese Ropes, a sort of leg twisting thing done with knotted elastic bands; Best Falls, where one of us would 'shoot' the rest and the one who executed the most elaborate and protracted death scene would win and be the shooter next time around.

Our local newsagent started selling something called a Footsie - a small plastic hoop with a string and ball attached. You put the hoop round one ankle and spun it, jumping over the string with the other foot. Once mastered, you could Footsie for miles and forget the way home. If you couldn't afford the official plastic gizmo, we discovered you could make a slightly clunkier version with a tennis ball tied inside one of your mother's stockings and tied round your leg.

We played straightforward Hide and Seek and Chap the Door and Run Away, though we developed our own version of the latter because we couldn't quite get to our hiding places on time and kept getting caught. So we would tie a length of black thread to the door knocker and pull the thread from the safety of our hiding places. Re-sult.

Two teams of us would line up opposite each other holding hands. One team would call a person from the other side by shouting:

"Red Rover, Red Rover we call so-and-so over."

That person would run head first into the opposite line and use their weight, brute force, tickling, farting, biting... pretty much anything to break the chain.

British Bulldog was a game where one person (usually the biggest) would stand in the middle of our play area. They were the bulldog and everyone else stood at the other. When the bulldog shouted 'go' we would all try to run to the other end without getting caught by the bulldog. If you were caught you became an extra bulldog and helped out in the next round. The main bulldog would then shout 'Go' and we'd all run the other way, back and forth till there was only one person left – that was, the winner.

We played Blind Man's Bluff, Tag, Conkers, Kiss Chase, Marbles or Bools, Rounders and Football. We'd fish for tadpoles and collect frogs and newts which we kept in rubber-banded shoe boxes on the top of our wardrobes. We'd doggy paddle in the dam that served the old Cotton Mill. I don't recall ever being taught to swim, but we improvised our own, perfectly functional, version.

The heavy, seven foot wooden washing poles were the most versatile of props and consequently, featured in all manner of make believe. There was one game that inevitably involved a beheading and that took place on top of one of the flat tombs in the local graveyard. Washing poles made brilliant jousting poles and if you could persuade your Da or one of your older brothers to nail a couple of bits of wood onto two washing poles, you had a most excellent pair of stilts.

The long hot summers of the early 70's were carefree and happy. Sun-freckled and smelling of good old fresh air, we romped our way round the estate.

Our older brother Davey would sometimes deign to join in our games. But he would generally go too far, grabbing kids roughly at Bulldog and Tag, pushing them over at Blind Man's Bluff and twisting kids' arms in a Chinese burn at Red Rover.

His version of Hide and Seek was Hide-and-No-Seek. He'd send the younger kids off to hide then – whistling - head off home. Eventually they'd re-emerge to find there was no-one there.

He'd look at the girls in a way I can only describe as predatory. They sensed it too and in his presence, drew together for safekeeping.

Washing poles weren't play weapons in Davey's hands. He played for real. After many rounds of black eyes, broken teeth and one broken jaw, the other kids wouldn't play with us as they were too scared of Davey.

Mam swore to the police that Davey couldn't know he was 'endangering lives' when he found a tatty old stuffed dog on wheels, removed the wheels and placed the dog on the sharp, blind bend where the buses turned into the terminus. The drivers – thinking on first glance it was a real dog - would slam on the brakes, the buses would skid and any remaining passengers would be thrown from their seats. Davey was eventually pulled from his hiding place and brought home grinning in the back of a police van.

Mam said Roddy and I were 'thick as thieves'. Davey was one. A thief, I mean. He started small – just some polo mints and tubes of smarties from Galbraiths. He progressed to bottles of perfume and bubble bath sets from the chemist shop on the corner of the parade which he then sold around the estate. Many a mother received a *choried* bottle of Je Reviens on Mothering Sunday.

After the police brought Davey back from yet another of his sprees, Dad knew he was obliged to act, for our code said it was the man's job to discipline.

As he reached for his belt, Mam interjected:

"Phil. He's just a wean. He'll grow out of it."

Would it have made any difference if Mam had allowed Dad to act? Probably not. I suspect Davey was already beyond help.

Twice a year 'the shows' came to the large expanse of waste ground by the brick factory. A convoy of mud-caked lorries dragging rusty caravans or clanking trailers would clatter into view and begin the setting up of the much anticipated stalls and rides. Rumour had it they would give kids free rides when they were testing, but I know of not one case where that actually happened.

Davey, Roddy and I would each be given just one 50p coin to spend at the shows. That equated to five rides each.

I can still smell the hamburgers and the candy floss and hear the thump, thump, thump of the bass on the huge bin speakers, the continuous hum of the generators and the rapid bam, bam of the air rifles.

Bare chested, tattoo-ed, testosterone-emboldened traveller youths competed to entice the punters to jump onto the Speedway, the Waltzers, the Dodgems and the Cyclone Twist. Once they'd filled their seats, they would yell:

"Dis anybody want tae go faster?"

And breathless, saucer-eyed kids would scream:

"**Meeeeeeeeeeeee**.........."

The older girls from the estate would lean on the rides' support pillars, chew their Chiclets and stare longingly at these muscled, tattoo-ed gods, dreaming of the day they might elope with a showman. I can't say I heard of that happening either.

I remember clearly the songs that blasted from the individual rides and melded into one glorious, discordant mash up:

Alice Cooper *'Schools Out;'* Chicory Tip *'Son of My Father'*; T'Rex *'Metal Guru'*; Slade *'Take Me Back 'Ome'*; Rod Stewart *'You Wear it Well'*; Lieutenant Pigeon *'Mouldy Old Dough'*; Slade *'Mama We're All Crazy Now'*; Chuck Berry *'My Ding A Ling'*; Jimmy Osmond *'Long Haired Lover from Liverpool'*.

For Roddy and I, our 50p was spent all too soon, but Davey hooked up with the tattoo-ed gods and got himself free rides on the Waltzers by helping spin the cars. A privilege he didn't share with his younger siblings who, having run out of money, were just hanging about, drinking in the carnival atmosphere.

We estate kids were both fascinated and repelled by the larger-than-life show people. It was rumoured that they stole and sold babies, that they could do magic, invoke curses and see into the future.

For the two weeks the shows were on the waste ground, we were given to understand that the younger show kids would attend the local schools. We couldn't wait to rub shoulders with these wild and darkly exotic creatures. Alas, it didn't happen. Those jammy Feen-yins got them all.

Every summer, almost as soon as the schools broke up for the holidays, a charity called 'Happy Days' would come to our estate, collect around thirty under-tens and take them to the seaside.

The year I turned nine and Roddy seven, we were chosen. We could scarcely sleep the night before, having never been on holiday or seen the sea.

The following morning we lined up with the other kids, each of us clutching plastic bags or kiddy-sized suitcases, plus footballs or small net-bagged spades and pails.

At 9 a.m. three twelve-seater Bedford minibuses came into view, trailing multi-coloured balloons and streamers, horns tooting. Each bus had a driver and a volunteer in fancy dress. Our driver was called Uncle Boaby and our volunteer was an acne-d, clown-suited teenager called Rachel. In we piled, racing for the back of the bus, our voices shrill with excitement. As we drove the hour and a half to Heads of Ayr, Rachel led us in a whole raft of songs. We gave it our all.

"The frr....**ont** of the bus they canny sing..." "Three wee craws sat upoan a wa'" "Ye cannae shove yer granny aff a bus...." "Ally Bally, Ally Bally Bee...." "One Two Three Aleerie...." "Skinny Malinky long legs, big banana feet...." "Murder, murder polis, three stairs up...." "Bee Baw Babbity..." "Ah've goat a sausage..." "Ma Auntie Mary hud a canary.." "Ma Maw's a Millionaire..."

Eventually we ran out of songs. But just as wee Danny Lawson burst into a hoarse rendition of "Away in a Manger..." we hit the coast road and caught our first glimpse of the sea. And that's when Rachel really ramped up the excitement.

We were going to somewhere called Butlins Holiday Camp where we would stay for three whole days. As we approached,

Rachel read from a long list of all the amazing things we could do there. And what a list it was.

Rachel shouted:

"There's a gi-normous helter skelter".

Uncle Boaby shouted:

"How much does that cost?"

Rachel shouted "It's **FREEEEE**!!!"

Rachel shouted:

"There's a huge heated swimming pool."

Uncle Boaby shouted "How much does that cost?"

Rachel responded:

"It's **FREEEEEE**!!!!!"

By now, we kids had caught on to the game.

Rachel called out the names of the attractions, we shouted "How much does that cost?" and Rachel responded "It's **FREEEEE**!"

By the time she'd worked her way through the whole list – dodgems, merry go-round, go-carts, roller skating rink, swimming pool, competitions, fancy dress, It's a Knockout, Pirate Hunt, ice cream and donkey rides – we were in a state of almost hysteria. Could we really do all this for free?

As we rolled up to the gate and were signed in, we were each given a map of the site with the location of the various 'camps' plus all the attractions.

Roddy and I held hands and joined the other kids who were gaping in wide-eyed wonder. The streets were immaculate – no cigarette butts, broken bottles, litter or dog shit. An abundance of flowers spilled from grass verges and an assortment of tubs and planters – geraniums, miniature roses, lillies, poppies, begonias and marigolds. A heavenly scent drifted on the breeze.

A posh sounding lady's voice boomed from the crackly tannoy:

"**Hullooo** campers! Today's programme includes Miss Lovely Legs; the Bonny Baby Competition; Glamorous Grannies; under-10's disco; Star Trail Talent Competition; Sunsilk Hair Competition; Clown Around at the Gaiety Theatre; Prize Bingo; Tombola; Melody Maker Singing Competition; and Fancy Dress at the Beachcomber Bar.

And head on over for It's a Knockout, Punch and Judy, the Scavenger Hunt and our glorious Holiday Princess Competition on the Gaiety Green. Don't miss the Sunshine Parade by our talented Red Coat Revue Company. And boys and girls....don't forget to pick up your Beaver Club badges!"

The kids from our estate were in 'Yellow Camp'. Accompanied by our volunteers, we were to sleep in 'Chalets'. They were basically oversized garden sheds with shoogly, squeaky metal beds, but to us, they were magical tree houses.

Four kids to each chalet, they had mixed Proddies and Feen-yins with what might have been seen as irresponsible abandon. I suspect they'd done that deliberately, but I've no proof that that was their intention. Astonishingly, it didn't seem to matter.

Each day, three huge meals would be provided and on day one, we arrived in plenty time for Yellow Camp's allocated slot - the midday sitting in the vast dining hall. The food was remarkably similar to our free school meals – in other words, drop dead brilliant – and we each had a huge bowl of vanilla, chocolate and strawberry ice-cream with two fan wafers and hundreds and thousands to finish.

After lunch we were given our programmes and let loose. There was a high wire fence around the whole complex to ensure that we didn't leave the park... Seriously?....Why would anyone leave the park?

Late afternoon, we got changed in the little poolside cabins below the huge sign that said 'Our Intent is Your Delight'. I had a too-tight blue nylon 'bubble' bathing suit which left a deep red welt around the top of my thighs and Roddy had some chunky knitted trunks that would constantly slide down with the weight of the water. We joined hordes of screaming kids intent on pushing Red Coat 'pirates' from the diving boards.

Each evening, the Red Coats would put on a show. When they shouted "Anyone from Glasgow?" we waved like crazy and screamed ourselves hoarse. From time to time a light that said 'Baby Crying' would flash above the performers' heads and someone in the audience would scuttle off.

At the skating rink, we handed over our chalet keys and were given roller skates in our shoe size. Laughing Red Coats taught us how to balance and skate in wobbly circles and by the end of day two, Roddy and I had found our balance and were zig zagging and skating backwards.

In the afternoon of the third day, the camp gates were opened and we piled out onto the beach.

From our reading, Roddy and I were sure we'd got the measure of this place called the seaside. We had not. The reality was a full-blown assault on every one of our senses.

We were entranced by the epic force of the waves, the sharp, briny scent on the air, the plaintive screeching of gulls, the visceral squelch of warm, wet sand as it oozed up between our toes and the shimmering mystery of what lay beyond the vast haze of the horizon.

I asked Rachel what the large, visible island was.

"Oh that's Arran, Debs. Spectacular views, eh?"

"A-mazing! And what lies on the other side of the island?"

"That – young Debs – would be America".

Once changed into our 'swimmers', our group scattered across the beach. Some chased the crabs that scurried toward the retreating waves and then away from the waves as they crashed to shore.

Others built wobbly sandcastles, rushing back and forward filling pails of water to compact the sand and fill their moats. Rachel showed them how to make little flags by sticking bits of twig through leaves.

Roddy and I, with Rachel and a couple of other kids took our pails and headed for the rock pools.

"Careful not to cast a shadow over the pool" said Rachel. "The wee beasties will think you're a predator and they'll run and hide!"

Peering into the pools we saw tiny, scuttling crabs, miniature darting fish, green, slimy seaweed with lots of what looked like blisters, mussels, limpets and little spiral shells moving slowly on the bottom of the pool.

"Those are hermit crabs" said Rachel. "They make their homes in empty shells left by other wee animals and as they grow they find themselves new, bigger houses."

Roddy tried to pick up one of the limpets.

"Ooooh...those little guys cling on so hard Roddy, that they actually leave an impression in the rock."

Rachel picked up some pieces of sea glass and showed them to me.

"These" she whispered "are what mermaids use to make their jewellery."

Behind us, a group of kids were trying to bury each other in the sand. Another group went charging into the water, their gleeful expressions turning to surprise as the sharp chill of the water registered on their tender regions.

Uncle Boaby inflated a beach ball which caught on the breeze and barrelled down the length of the beach followed by a screaming horde of kids.

"Watch out for the jellyfish, you lot!" yelled Uncle Boaby.

Eventually, emotionally exhausted, bedraggled, sun kissed and wind burnt, we schlepped back to camp in time to shake out the sand and dry ourselves for dinner.

All too soon our holiday was at an end. Our tummies full and our heads overflowing with the happiest of memories, we queued up with our little red Butlins autograph books to collect the signatures of the performers and the Red Coats.

The precious gift that Happy Days gave the estate kids was Time Out. Time out from chores and responsibilities. Time out from the relentless corrosiveness of the adults' bitterness and thwarted sense of entitlement. Mostly though, it was time out from our inherited, thankless and pointless task of perpetuating sectarian hate. We knew what we were and what we had to do. We were apprentice bigots and as long as we were on the estate, we did our duty.

Away from the estate, away from the adults, we were allowed to be thirty, normal, excited kids having fun in the sun.

CHAPTER 3 - JESUS SAVES

Happy Days being the only welcome exception, our estate was overrun with what the adults referred to as bleeding hearts and bloody do-gooders.

These wannabee saviours spewed forth from various churches, charities, educational institutions and voluntary organisations. There was even a time when we were graced by a visit from His Royal Highness 'Big Ears'. We didn't want him of course, but no-one thought to ask what we wanted.

I remember particularly Miss Lilly, a young visiting teacher from a Christian Mission in Kent. She assured us all that while "we were broken", we were not to worry. God had sent her to fix us.

The general consensus was that little actual good was ever done, that we were studied in endless, intrusive and insulting detail and consulted on not very much. To be fair, most, or perhaps all reasonable suggestions that were proffered were generally rejected out of hand, the better to safeguard the anti-establishment mythology of the tribe.

In the Autumn of '73, however, two new strangers appeared. And to me at least, it seemed they were far more interesting than the usual suspects.

They were introduced to me via an unlikely source - Mima Corrigan and Linda Kelty – our two token female bullies. Said bullies were showing off a collection of oversized embroidered motifs and badges on their school bags and uniforms. There were rainbows, really cool peace signs and what looked like Coca-Cola badges.

"Oooh, **niiice**..." I said, tentatively, for I was never too sure of my ground.

"Where'd you get those?"

On closer inspection I noticed they all had a religious sub-text – "Jesus Christ the Real Thing", "Jesus Saves" and "I Am the Way the Truth and The life."

"Coupla daft weirdos down the Community Centre. Giving loads of them out for free."

The following evening, intrigued, but expecting nothing more than a few freebies, I found myself perched on one of the Community Centre's wobbly plastic chairs.

I will admit that the newcomers did fall into the hated category of do-gooders, but these guys were different. They came from Alabama for a start . . . . and not a banjo in sight.

Norris, The group leader was bland, bald and somewhat forgettable. His partner could only be described as a revelation. His name was Wilson and despite taking his name from a well-known make of football, he was the most engaging and exotic male I'd had the pleasure to encounter.

His eyes were a deep, piercing blue. His skin had a soft sallowness and his hair was thick, curly and glossy. I suspect he had a touch of the Latino about him, but whatever was the case, he was the most beautiful, shiny and wholesome looking man I'd ever seen.

His voice was soft and engaging. Every word carefully chosen, kind, thoughtful and reflective.

They were evangelists. Come to spread the Word amongst the non-engaged, the great unsaved and – of course – the great unwashed.

You could say we already 'had' religion. But I would say that, strictly speaking, we did not.

When Wilson spoke of his relationship with Jesus, his eyes shone and he looked Heavenward, as though transported to that other, most perfect realm.

"Jesus said, love thy neighbour as thyself."

"Jesus said, forgive those who have wronged you."

"Jesus said, love your enemies."

"Jesus said, do unto others as you would have them do unto you."
"Jesus said, love one another as I have loved you."

I hung on Wilson's every word. As the clouds of ignorance and mediocrity lifted, a searing shaft of enlightenment entered my very being. Each story was a perfect capsule of beauty, it's meaning clear and compelling. For the first time, I felt I'd encountered someone who lived out and embodied his professed beliefs. I hadn't heard religion presented in this way – not as an unthinking, automatic tribal adherence - but as a profound moral code, a personal voyage of discovery.

I'd inherited a set of dull, tawdry, banal and not-to-be-challenged restrictions and sectarian regulations. But Wilson's authentic witness made religion make actual sense. It was immediate and it was beautiful. I didn't know that this was what Christianity was. I most certainly didn't know that this was what being a Proddy or a Feen-yin was supposed to be about.

I lived for the meetings and each weekend I set off with the growing band of evangelicals to various street corners where the Americans would play their guitars and we would sing our hearts out and bang our tambourines.

For once, Mam resisted sarcastic remarks and scathing comments. But if she saw me on the street with them, she pursed her lips, turned her face and crossed the road.

I didn't care. I was gone. I'd never experienced such total bliss.

My belief was entire, my heart full, my life infused with vital meaning. I **belonged**.

For months, I basked in the glory of Wilson's presence. When he spoke, it was only to me. The sun was warm on my face and everything spoke of Heaven. Wilson even smelled of Heaven. Though with hindsight, I'm guessing it was cologne.

About five months in, Wilson took me aside.

"It's time" he said. "The Lord has spoken to me and He tells me you're ready to accept the Holy Spirit."

I'd heard of the Holy Spirit but only in connection with the impregnation of Mary in the Nativity story. Nonetheless, I wasn't afraid, as I needed no convincing that Wilson wanted only the best for me.

"Go home, be alone and pray" he said. "The Spirit will come to you."

And so I did. I prayed some. I prayed some more. And then some more. But nothing happened. I believed like I'd never believed in anything before. I wanted it more than anything I'd ever wanted. But it didn't happen. I tried to convince myself I felt different. Renewed. Reborn. Full of something that hadn't been there.

But I didn't.

I stayed in my room for days. Didn't eat. Cried and cried. Eventually I accepted that I'd imagined belonging to something that wasn't real for me, that didn't want me. I wished with all my heart that it did. But it wasn't to be. I had been rejected.

Mam rolled her eyes, shook her head and muttered:

"Cry on Mrs. Simpson. Everything's al-ways about **you**."

Wilson knocked on our door many times over the following weeks, but there was no route back for me. Only emptiness, loneliness and the agony of false promises.

I was to make many attempts in the years that came after to re-enter that state of total bliss. And I think it's fair to say, I've left few stones unturned in that search.

◆ ◆ ◆

When I was fourteen I took the first step towards financial independence. I secured a job as a Saturday girl at Curl-up-N-Dye, a hair salon at the opposite end of the parade from the chemist shop. This salon was strictly for old ladies and smelled of mothballs and Fisherman's Friends.

For an eight hour shift I earned the princely sum of three pounds. With the thrift honed from maximising the value of the penny tray, three pounds bought untold riches. A little bit of make-up, the occasional polyester top from Kumar's, the Jackie magazine, clip on earrings, packets of Munchies and Mintola and the joss sticks that Mam hated.

The weekly hairdo was a big event for the estate's pensioners. They'd arrive, chattering excitedly, their best hats secured by oversized hat pins to what was left of last week's hairdo and their best brooches pinned to their cardi's.

For the estate's women, long hair over forty was an absolute no-no. It meant you were still 'chasing men'. The ubiquitous head of short sausage curls was the only way to go and that made life oh so easy at the salon.

Each Saturday, just before opening, I would set out a row of bottles in the back shop. Hidden from the customers' view, I would take a funnel and decant the big plastic two-gallon containers of cheap shampoo and coloured rinses from Salon Select wholesalers into the pretty, one-purchase-only designer bottles.

When the ladies arrived, I would take the wee fat coats, still warm from their owners, and hang them on the rail in the back shop. I would drape the ladies in their gowns, settle them down over the backwash basin and once they'd stopped fussing, try to wash what was left of their hair without scalding them or soaking their cardi's.

I loved our old biddies. We had some real characters.

Mrs. Derillo had a shock of white hair and sported a slash of scarlet lipstick which inevitably bled into the deep crevices which led down from nose to top lip. She insisted on cradling Darling, her pink-eyed, white-haired Maltese poodle while her 'do' was being done. Darling's mean little teeth snapped at any hands that got too close to 'mammy'.

Mrs. Thomas, whose mouth worked incessantly without producing much sound, would reach a dry hand into the deepest recesses of the patch pockets on her tweed coat and produce unwrapped, fluff-covered pan drops which stank of Woodbines. "One for each of the girls".

Mrs. Reilly, with her tartan carpet bag and dowager's hump, had a wooden walking stick carved with trailing leaves and thistles. She'd wink at us and use the stick to poke Darling when Mrs. Derillo wasn't looking.

When they queued up at the reception desk to pay, the old ladies were like rabbits in the headlights. They could scarcely cope with decimalisation and, with a sigh of either petition or resignation, they'd hand over their purses for us to remove the requisite amount of notes and coins.

Mrs. Reilly's purse was bound with several thick, tightly wound elastic bands and attached with a thick chain and an oversized nappy pin to the inside pocket of her apron. Extracting payment was a particularly slow and painful wrestle. When I reached the end of my patience, I would hear Mrs. Barr's voice in my head:

"Come oan you lot. Ah huvnae **goat** a' day."

At pay-time, Mrs. Derillo had her own version of difficult. She was entirely convinced we'd taken the opportunity of decimalisation to hike up our prices. We were just as certain we were there or thereabouts. We couldn't find a way to convince Mrs. Derillo, so we settled on a secret 'discount', just for her.

There was, I'm ashamed to say, one appointment I dreaded. Every Saturday at 2 p.m., quiet-spoken, rosy-cheeked Mrs. Graham would arrive to have her thin hair fluffed up as much as possible to hide the moonscape of cysts which covered her scalp.

Settling her gently onto the backwash, I would steady myself and take deep breaths as I tried not to show my discomfort. Mrs. Graham would chatter away and I would try to answer her between breaths.

I rubbed her scalp as gingerly as I could, the better to scoot over and not feel the undulations. Mrs. Graham reassured me:

"Scrub as hard as you like young Debs. They lumps don't hurt."

After a pink, blue or purple rinse and a session under the drier, she'd venture back out onto the street. As she left, she'd reach into her pinny and hand me a coin wrapped in paper.

"Just a wee somethin' for ye hen. Ye're such a bonny wee thing."

50p. That was a lot of money from a pensioner. I didn't want to accept it, not sure that post the evil that was decimalisation, she had any sense of how much money that actually was. But I do think she was grateful for my discretion. And my strong stomach.

Curl-up-N-Dye had a bank of hooded hairdryers along one wall. The old ladies would snuggle down into the squashy chairs, knitting or reading their magazines, sucking on their dentures and shouting to each other over the noise of the dryers.

If they nodded off on account of the heat, sometimes their mottled, spurtle-like legs would relax open, revealing oversized flannelette pantaloons and thick lisle stockings.

One Saturday, when Mrs. Graham's dryer clicked off, I tapped on the dryer hood to waken her. She slumbered on. I shook her softly by the shoulder. Nothing. Mrs. Graham was gone.

I went to fetch Irene, her hairdresser.

"What is it Debs? I'm right in the middle of a perm here."

Turning so the other old ladies couldn't see me, I rolled my eyes towards Mrs. Graham and drew my upturned palm under my chin.

"Oh *shit*" mouthed Irene.

When the realisation of what had just happened hit home, the salon was in an uproar. The old biddies squirmed out from under their driers and stood gaping at them, willing the machines to offer up explanations and answers.

"Ah telt her she was lacing them stays o' hers far too tight" said Mrs. Thomas.

"Nah. Ah blame that wee Frankie" said Mrs. Reilly. "Ye know Frankie, aye? He's that sexy wee bag o'muscle takes the Fit for Life classes doon the Community Centre? Fair gets the auld yins hearts beatin' faster."

An ear-splitting **mee-maw** was heard and a panda car with flashing blue lights screeched to a halt in front of the salon. To the old biddies' immense satisfaction, it seemed that there was to be a '**po-lis** investigation'. After a week of intense speculation that was building to a most ridiculous and hysterical crescendo, a lovely policewoman called Betty came to reassure us.

"It wasn't anything you did. Her heart just gave out. Her time had come."

Jesus might not have saved Mrs. Graham, but I did hope that whoever had taken her away had taken out her rollers and backcombed what was left of her tresses.

◆ ◆ ◆

Irene and I travelled to Linn Crematorium to join the crowd of family and friends gathered for Mrs. Graham's funeral service. The funeral notice in the Daily Record asked mourners to wear a piece of blue ribbon.

Mrs. Graham's granddaughter Abi read the eulogy:

"My Nan as you all know was a happy, smiling and hugely loving woman. She was a good wife and mammy, went to church regularly and had a kind word for everyone. She put her kids, her family, her neighbours.... everyone before herself.

She brought up four kids in a one room and a kitchen, three floors up in a crumbling Govan tenement with no bathroom, just one cold, ancient, shared toilet on the landing that everyone in the whole close had to use. They didn't have toilet paper, just ripped up pieces of newspaper to wipe themselves. The smaller kids couldn't reach the chain to flush so they'd have to climb up onto the toilet seat and risk falling in.

In the daytime they could see the spiders and the mice that ran under the toilet door. And that was scary enough. At night they could only imagine. The kids were too scared to go, so they would all use the potty in the night and queue up with all the other families in the morning to slop it out.

There was no hot running water. Nan washed herself and the kids in the deep kitchen sink, the same sink in which she would peel the potatoes and do the weekly wash. She told us her hands would often break out in sores from the scrubbing and from the harsh carbolic soap.

When they didn't have enough shillings to put in the electric meter they'd boil the kettle and cook the meals on the coal fire.

All four kids slept in a three quarters bed in the kitchen recess, two at the top and two at the bottom, with ginger bottles filled with hot water at their feet and the whole family's coats on top of the blankets in the winter months.

When the kids got a bit bigger and went to school, Nan would go out and clean the big houses in Whitecraigs.

When the news came through that Nan had got to the top of the queue for a new council flat on the estate with three rooms and an inside bathroom, she felt she'd got herself a palace. She was over the moon.

My Nan was a strong woman and she never complained. As I said, she put everyone else first. We would buy nice things for her – new bedclothes, new curtains, new china . . . all sorts of things. But she wouldn't use them. She just put them in the cupboard for someone else to have when she died.

In the last few years though it seemed as though she realised she didn't have long. She starting living for herself. She'd meet her pals at the bingo, go to her Fit for Life classes down the Community Centre and she'd treat herself to a weekly shampoo and set at the hairdressers. She joined a local writing group and started to write poetry. This is one of the last pieces she wrote. It's called 'The Blue Ribbon'.

When I peer into the mirror
This creature that I see
The stoop, the lines, the lifeless hair
How can she be me?

Come closer and I'll tell you
Of a life less lived
The places I did not get to
The joys not in my gift

The girl with the blue ribbon
Bouncing curls and sparkling eyes
Lives within me still - and asks me why?
When I've yet to live, why must I now lay down and die?"

Abi – eyes brimming – swallowed and took a moment to recover her composure.

"We – the family, wish she'd had more of those special years. We will miss her. We love you Nan."

I too wished better for Mrs. Graham. I wished she'd run off as a girl and travelled the world. I wished she'd lived her life. I wished she'd just said no to what was expected, to a life of servitude with no discernible purpose.

I thought about my own gran. She'd told me remarkably similar stories about eking out a living in the miserable squalor that was the Gorbals. Her family and her neighbours' families were packed in like sardines, sometimes up to eight to a room. Sometimes the rooms were so small they'd have to sleep in shifts.

The rat-infested drains would constantly overflow and excrement spill into the alleyways where the kids played. Up to thirty people shared one outside tap and a stinking toilet with only half a door. Broken windows were patched with cardboard. Gran told how they would hide from the landlord's men when they came to collect the overdue rent. They would try to keep the gas lights going in the night, for, under cover of darkness, the rats grew bolder.

Women would routinely bear a child a year, often up to twelve or thirteen in total. Some of those might die of scarlet fever, whooping cough, pneumonia or smallpox.

I don't remember all that much about Gran since she died when I was young. But I do remember one angry exchange between her and Mam when I was maybe five or six.

"What is it you **want** Beryl?" Gran had yelled. "Why is this lovely new hoose, a hard-working man and these three gorgeous weans not enough for you? Is there anything that would actually make you happy?"

The answer, as yet, appeared to be no. Mam's life choices had left her disappointed, angry, disillusioned and bitter. Yet she envisaged – no actually seemed to want – the same outcome for me. And that was never going to happen.

CHAPTER 4 - SEX AND DRUGS
AND ROLL-YOUR-OWNS

Cast adrift and inconsolable after the Great Spiritual Let-Down, distraction if not rescue turned up in the form of my new best friend Caz.

Having caved at last to the avalanche of accusations and rumours, the parish authorities had relocated Bill and family to faraway Shetland. It was with the heaviest of hearts I'd said goodbye to Mhairead, confident we'd remain best friends forever. We wrote regularly, but it wasn't the same. Proximity is everything and we didn't have social media then.

I met Caz at the library where she'd just been wowing all assembled at the local drama club.

"Hey... I haven't seen you before!" she said. "Come join us. We're always looking for new blood."

I drew back. I wasn't exactly overflowing with confidence.

"No. No thanks, really. It's just not my thing."

I was astonished that Caz chose me as a friend. Caz was everything I wanted to be. Brash, sassy and brimming with brio, she lit up every room.

Caz had pink hair when no-one had pink hair. She had tattoos and piercings at a time when it was considered provocatively rebellious. Her clothes were a discordant riot of tie dye, tribal prints, patchwork denim and cheesecloth. Caz was a phenomenon. Caz didn't follow the rules.

Davey gave a long, low whistle when he saw me out on the street with Caz.

"**Man**...she's a bit of alright."

Caz rolled her eyes and threw him a withering 'when hell freezes over' stare.

Caz's parents lived just outside our estate in a development of high flats. Not council exactly, but run by something called a housing association.

Her dad Jonathan was subdued and generally rather unremarkable. He wore faded, shapeless grey suits and worked nine to five in some minor local government capacity.

He'd carefully close the car door at 5.25 pm precisely each evening, remove his tie and fold it in three, then bash out the most energetic and life-affirming honky tonk and jazz piano for exactly half an hour. Then he'd shroud himself once more in his habitual greyness and retire to the rear side of a newspaper for the rest of the evening. It was a bizarre and entirely fascinating ritual.

Caz's mum Maureen was Carmen Miranda to his Mr. Bleh. Shrill and vivacious, she'd plastered their modest, anonymous flat with dramatic murals of palm-fringed beaches and furnished it with futons, orange plastic chairs and voluminous jumbo cord bean bags. Clad always in garish vintage tribal print mumus and with her trademark vibrant slash of orange lipstick, Maureen could often be found sprawled at floor level sucking on the last centimetre or so of a joint, patchouli and jasmine joss sticks smoking in a variety of vessels.

Caz had a brother Nigel who might have helped me overcome my obsession with Wilson had he not been – forgive my Francaise - such a total dick.

He had the look of a stoned Messiah about him – not, as we've said, that Jesus could have conceivably been white.

Summer or winter, Nigel's uniform of choice was a faded kaftan, Birkenstocks and a top hat.

At first I'd try to get his attention – have him confirm my existence with a 'hi' or even just a nod. He ignored me and he ignored Caz. She didn't seem to mind, but I seethed internally.

Four years older than us, he endured his early morning shifts as a postman as they freed him up for the rest of the day to listen to music, drop tabs and hammer out some endlessly repetitive riffs on his pawn shop bought Stratocaster. At weekends he and the four other much feted members of 'The Aptness' set up not-entirely-legal gigs in odd places such as disused warehouses and graveyards.

Between you and me, he wasn't especially gifted. But when you're in a band and you look as he did, actual talent would be somewhat of a bonus.

Nigel broke with all reasonable expectation in that he didn't have one girlfriend at a time. He had several and if they were each aware of it, they didn't appear to mind. One in particular – Mia – fascinated me. She was a tiny, bird like Thai girl with massive eyes and a glorious smile. I wanted to get close to her, but Nigel protected everything in his stable from the likes of me or Caz. Or so he thought.

Nigel (never Nige) was most particular about his hi-fi equipment. Caz seemed pretty knowledgeable about what was what in the Hi-Fi echelons and she talked me through the pros and pros of the Linn Sondek LP12, the NAD 320 amplifier and Acoustic Research speakers.

When he wasn't out rutting, Nigel would spend countless hours making minute adjustments to the position and height of his speakers, the suspension and the height of the arm on the deck and the precise, exquisite balance of the stereophonic sound.

Nigel's saving grace was his glorious taste in music. When he wasn't home, Caz and I would sneak into his bedroom – all psychedelia and Hendrix posters – lie on his much-guarded bed and select sleeve after sleeve of iconic concept albums that filled the room with vast, almost circular sound and profound reverberations.

He had prog rock tours de force from the crème de la crème of iconic bands – Floyd, King Crimson, Cream, ELP, Tull, Rush, Caravan, Hawkwind, Zeppelin, Uriah Heep, Tangerine Dream, Deep Purple, Gong, Wishbone Ash, Barclay James Harvest, Pendragon.... oh I could go on.

Though it was difficult not to baulk at what this assembly must have cost, I couldn't deny the exquisite, pin-drop quality of the sound. It ruined for me the tinky-tinky rattle of Da's Amstrad tower cabinet, bought on 24-month hire purchase from Woolworths. Da's bland Elton John and Wings albums lost all appeal. I'm ashamed to say I did become quite the hi-fi snob.

When each of our illicit listening sessions ended, Caz and I carefully replaced every item as it had been for, had Nigel become aware of our incursions, he'd make damn sure they weren't repeated.

◆ ◆ ◆

Caz and her friends acquired their style from flea markets or a local alternative boutique called Karma. Since Karma didn't take the Provi (no shit!) and Mam refused to spend money on 'manky looking hippy gear', Caz passed on what she outgrew. As luck would have it, her figure developed early and her new curves strained at the seams of her old kaftans and Brutus jeans.

Posing before my mirror in Caz's cast offs, I saw in my reflection someone who had donned the mantle of someone else's choices. Not because the clothes didn't fit – they hung quite nicely if I'm honest. But because, try as I might, I couldn't carry them off with the pizzazz Caz did.

One item I coveted – and was eventually given – was a rancid old Afghan coat which Mam said made our house stink of wet dog. It did – stink I mean - but I loved the way I looked in it.

Mam muttered under her breath something about 'cast offs from scroungers and dirty layabouts'. I felt a sharp stab of pain on my friends' behalf. I pretended I had no idea what she meant. I did know if I'm honest, but I didn't want to know. When the summer came round again and I wasn't wearing the coat, it had somehow found itself another home.

We – Caz and co. - regarded ourselves as alternative, a bit 'out there'. But between you and me, there was a detectable element of conformity to our choices. Sartorial options were limited almost exclusively to denim, cheesecloth, velvet and tie dye. Perfume was Jasmine and Patchouli. Footwear choice was Docs, Converse and Stocks. If I'm honest, we all pretty much conformed to the uniform of the non-conformist. Oh! The irony!

Caz would often have what she called 'gatherings'. Gatherings consisted of a bunch of random, seemingly unconnected people lying around listening to music, having intense conversations and partaking of a range of recreational drugs.

In the 70's, New Age experimentation with alternative spiritual movements and strange-seeming religious belief systems was on the increase. Acid, I was told, was **the** route to achieving the requisite mind-expansion.

From a fuzzy, eclectic hotch-potch of beliefs, we could choose from Holistic Divinities; semi-divine beings called angels or masters that humans could channel; UFO and cult 'religions' like Erich von Daniken's; Alternative Healing/Holistic Health movements; and all manner of mystical esotericism.

The virtual canonisation of rock legends like Hendrix, Joplin, the Stones and the Dead only served to fuel all manner of experimentation with hallucinogens. Weed use was so commonplace as to be almost dull, coke's star was rising and at the fringes of our group was a level of early experimentation with heroin.

Caz restricted her experimentation to smoking two or three joints a day, often with Maureen. She would proffer a drag but, try as I might, smoking made me choke. Concerned that I was missing out on something so life-affirming, Maureen baked a batch of cannabis laced cookies. They tasted rank and mouldy. I forced one down and waited patiently for some sort of effect. Nothing happened. Ab-solutely de **nada**. Given how foul they tasted – I wasn't tempted to choke another one down.

Caz was sixteen before I was and it was at that point she started disappearing off from time to time during the gatherings. Caz - she was thrilled to impart – was having sex. She would regale me with every lurid detail of the mechanics and I was both fascinated and repulsed in equal measure.

I didn't fancy it to say the least. And I guess when you uncouple sex from love and narrate the raw mechanics, there's every danger that it'll sound somewhat gross. And it did.

I wondered perhaps if I would have felt differently about the prospect of sex with someone I had feelings for. Wilson maybe? But no. Not Wilson. I was but a pubescent child then and my fascination with Wilson was akin to Bridie's with Jesus. I wanted it pure. Unsullied. *Idealistic.* **Uh oh.**

A regular at Caz's gathering was Erik. Erik was to be found on the fringes of a number of groupings. His father was a Norwegian who worked on the rigs and Erik had inherited his Viking blondeness and understated manliness.

Erik was the peacemaker. When disputes would kick off, Erik would flash his broad, dimpled, gap-toothed smile and lighten the mood with a well-chosen joke or a gentle, placatory comment.

And in those turbulent times, there was much to inspire conflict, confrontation and dissent. As the brave, free love ideologies of the 60's met the grim realities of life in the 70's, tempers flared. This one defended the miners' strikes, despite the black outs and economic hardships; another resented being held to ransom by unions.

Impassioned disputes would break out over women's rights, gay rights, Vietnam, who was the founding member of Lynrd Skynrd and which one wrote Freebird. Sometimes the 'mind expansion' tipped over into a level of anarchy. And in would step Erik.

I found myself more and more in Erik's company and – sharing a similar sense of humour – we became gradually closer, seeking one another out in the various groupings. Erik worked for a music promotion company and when he acquired a couple of freebies for a Sensational Alex Harvey Band gig at the Apollo he asked me to go with him.

I found my innards pleasantly aflutter at the prospect. I wasn't a fan of glam rock per se and I didn't especially enjoy the gig, but I did enjoy Erik's arm casually draped around my waist and the looks he shot me when he thought I wasn't looking.

Going forward we were always in each other's company. Laughing, talking well into the wee small hours. I felt I'd known him forever. I felt that we *belonged* together. I assumed those halcyon days would continue always and I felt warm and content.

Caz loved to joke about our relationship:

"**Babes**! Do you know what proportion of Scottish DNA there is in the Scandinavian gene pool? These guys have been abducting our women for centuries. And let's face it, who wouldn't go willingly?"

When Erik asked me into his bed I was strangely surprised. I hadn't thought of him that way. I hadn't thought about sex. I wasn't yet sixteen and far too young to be heading in that direction.

"But why not Debs? We know each other like we were born to be together, yes? I think about it all the time, being together with you in that way."

He looked entirely crestfallen at my lack of enthusiasm. I trotted out every objection I could muster – I'm too young; I don't know what to do; I could get pregnant. What I really meant was *I don't want to. I like things the way they are.*

We revisited this exchange a number of times and when it became clear he wasn't going to let this drop, I reluctantly agreed. I felt I'd lose him if I didn't. And how bad could it be?

Erik agreed to wear two condoms. I was tense. He was tense. His expectations were through the roof; I thought only of getting it over with.

In the end, it was over almost as soon as it begun. I could say perhaps he was inexperienced. But I wouldn't know.

His disappointment was palpable and I was unable to hide mine. My heart was in my shoes as we dressed and went our separate ways. The magic was gone, the sweetness, the innocence, replaced by a grim, almost grubby reality. I wished I'd stood my ground. But I expect he would have left me eventually. Perhaps his curiosity was too great or it may be that he felt love had to be cemented by and expressed through the physical. I don't know.

We still saw one another from time to time, but he could barely look me in the eye and it was all just hideously awkward. It was a long time before I'd consent to having sex again.

Erik aside, those were halcyon days. We revelled in some of the most intense and progressive music made before (or indeed since) and explored each other's minds without conclusion or thoughts of conclusion.

Looking back, the negative realisations took some time to dawn on me. Money was never discussed in our gatherings. It was seen as dirty, contaminating and unnecessary. We discussed all the prevailing causes - the environment, women's rights, gay rights, black rights, everyone's rights. Yet in a disconnected, almost academic way. As if we could cure the planet's ills by sucking on joints, dropping a few tabs and discussing the minutia of the government's and society's failures.

We saw ourselves as Social Justice Warriors I suppose, though we would not have deigned to attach any label to ourselves. Free as the birds we were.

To be honest, we were more like opposition politicians. Whatever 'they' (the establishment) were for, we were agin' it. Automatically and relentlessly. Therefore, you could say that 'they' set the agenda – theirs and ours. And you can't get more effective conformity than that.

It seems we expected everyone to be provided for and I heard it said more than once amongst our group that 'No-one should have to earn a living'. Being that if you're born, you automatically had a 'right' to a living and a good one at that.

Smoke, mirrors and semantics of course. That 'earning a living' was simply about something as ordinary and commonplace as paying your bills was conveniently ignored.

At no point did we discuss where the money came from for all that was expected and demanded. Nor indeed for the education and community facilities we enjoyed and for the welfare benefits that more than a few of our friends depended on.

And I've heard it implied many times since (and even now) that governments and local authorities 'have' money which they unreasonably withhold from this or that deserving group or cause. Where that money comes from – it would appear – is an unseemly, unsavoury and decidedly unglamorous topic.

Mam did inform me – with an unmistakeable note of satisfaction:

"That pal of yours – Nigel. He's dealing the drugs."

I shouldn't have been surprised. Nigel enjoyed a lifestyle that a part-time postie's wage would not support. But what did surprise me was the discovery that Caz was dealing too. I wasn't sure how I felt about that.

Not knowing what to think, I simply parked it.

CHAPTER 5 - MAZEL TOV

In the spring of my 16th year, an appointment was made for all year four pupils with Mr. Garry, the school Careers Officer. Mr. Garry was a weary, blotchy man with lank hair thrown into a reluctant comb over. His trademark threadbare corduroys were teamed with a garish Fair Isle tank top and his scuffed, slightly pointy shoes looped up at the front. Rumour had it that he was born without toes and stuffed newspaper in the fronts of his brogues.

When my turn came, he dropped into his chair with a sigh and produced dog-eared papers from a floppy satchel.

Whatever else he was, Mr. Garry was a realist. He was well aware that estate kids like me were expected to contribute to scant household incomes as soon as we were old enough to quit school. He knew that we were bred so that, in our own turn, we would populate and help sustain the tribe and its attendant mythology.

Still, I suppose he felt he had to ask:

"Sooo....Miss Gordon.....**Deborah**. Have you any thoughts perhaps about staying on at school? Your teachers speak so highly of you."

"Thanks. Everyone calls me Debs. And no – staying on's not really an option."

"Understood. Sooo ... any erm, career you're particularly drawn to?"

"Anything but factory work."

Mima and Linda, our local mean girls, had already joined the seamstressing ranks at the Playtex bra factory, earning the princely sum of £41 per week. In addition, they received 50%

off Cross Your Heart bras and Double Diamond girdles plus something called Luncheon Vouchers.

'Soooo.......anything in particular Debs that you **like** doing?"

I told him how I loved to write and that the previous year I'd come second in a national short story competition run by a well-known kids' cereal company. I'd also come first in a story writing competition sponsored by the local Chamber of Commerce. I remember receiving the Chamber award from our headmaster, Mr. Ambrose or 'Pierce' as he was more often called.

It was many years later that I discovered the apparent origin of the Mr. Ambrose's nickname. Tins of Ambrosia creamed rice at that time were designed to be boiled in a pot of water and I remember that there was an instruction on the lid that said 'Pierce here before boiling'. At least that's how the story goes.

"Actually Debs" – said Mr. Garry – "I have something here that just might interest you."

He scanned a short list on his desk headed up 'Current Vacancies'.

"It's an opening for a Junior Editorial Assistant with the Jewish Sentinel. Mostly pretty low level proof-reading and admin work initially, but some copy writing opportunities and no doubt a chance to move on to something bigger down the line. It doesn't pay much I'm afraid – just £17 a week."

Quickly recognising a potential implied criticism, he added:

"**All** newspaper jobs are low-paid at first of course."

I was hired on first interview. Mam was tight-lipped and furious.

"Mima" she said "bought her sister a top of the range Silver Cross pram with her first few week's wages."

I got the message.

Dad – while not angry as such – felt the need to proffer a warning: "Just watch yerself hen. The Yids look after their own."

I couldn't work out why that would be such a bad thing. Nor was I sure where Dad would have acquired knowledge of Jewish predilections. There were no Jews on the estate and I wasn't aware of having encountered Jews in any aspect of our usual life.

On reflection, I hadn't heard much hate speak or prejudice toward religions other than Catholic. But I guess we had our hands full hating them.

❖ ❖ ❖

The Sentinel was the key source of social, cultural and political news for the 15,000 or so Jews who had fled the Russian pogroms and the horrors of Nazi Germany to settle in Scotland.

Working for the Sentinel was a cultural revelation. The job itself wasn't especially challenging – mostly proof-reading, reception work and some low-level sales. But my sudden immersion in this closed, exotic world was as shocking as it was glorious.

The Editor Moshe Deichman was a gruff, grizzly, portly man in his late fifties with a generous heart and an endless stream of incomprehensible 'in' jokes. His office spilled over with dusty, yellowing paper and he hammered away most of the day on a battered Olivetti portable. On his desk were formal portraits of five handsome little Moshe clones. Each held a musical instrument – a cello, a flute, a bass clarinet, a violin and a double bass.

Moshe's office had a glass wall which allowed him to observe all office activities. An endless stream of rabbis and various community leaders came and went. Moshe would often be seen marching back and forward, gesticulating and pulling at what was left of his hair. I often wondered what they were discussing and only once – when the door was left slightly ajar – did I overhear:

"Seriously Chaim, this newspaper is no mouthpiece for your Zionist hate-speak. If I print, I print the truth."

Our sub-editor - Moshe's eldest son Natan – was a much more outgoing and affable character who ran a number of Jewish youth groups. His Catholic wife Ellen had converted to Judaism on their marriage the previous year.

While Moshe availed himself of the most obscure of Yiddish sayings, Natan peppered his speech with the more commonplace vernacular, almost as if he was playing a part in a film. He struck me as less authentic somehow, like those phony Scots in the Brigadoon film.

I was fascinated by the depth and range of the support groups that catered for every member of the community - Habonim, Betar, B'Nai Akiva, Jewish Welfare Board, Jewish Blind Society and Jewish Board of Guardians. I was particularly drawn to the idea of the Kibbutzim – my first introduction to the utopian concept of the collective community.

One of my main jobs was to sell Yarhzeit notifications. Each morning I would phone people with exotic and often difficult-to-pronounce names such as Azriel, Beirech, Chanoch, Tzeittel, Gisse, Dorzhe, Chizkiyahu and Rivkah and remind them that the anniversary of a loved one's death was approaching and that they might want to renew the memorial newspaper text for a further year.

They would rarely say no. Familial guilt made that particular selling job somewhat effortless. That's not to say I didn't get it wrong from time to time. One mother who was 'sadly missed' was mistyped as 'sadly pissed'. My next line of back up – Leo the linotype operator - missed it too. Or perhaps he chose to leave it in.

Natan laughed, a little too heartily in my opinion:

"**Jeez**. What a pair of *putzes*".

As the youngest member of the team, it fell to me to write the weekly music column. And – oh pinnacle of all that is joyous – this role came with complimentary concert tickets courtesy of the Glasgow Apollo.

I sat on the stairs with the emissaries from other newspapers and music magazines, proudly displaying my badge that said 'Press'. I had the privilege of seeing so many iconic artists and bands for free, including Barclay James Harvest, Caravan, 10CC, Thin Lizzy, The Ozark Mountain Daredevils, Santana, The Who, Lynrd Skynrd, Bob Marley, Genesis and Eric Clapton. There were some erm…less desirable gigs to cover - The Glitter Band, Lena Zavaroni, Ralph McTell and the Bay City Rollers. But – hey – life can't all be *sufganiyah*.

Although I was not of the Jewish community and I could grasp only limited chunks of what was happening around me, I can't say I was made to feel in any way excluded or unwelcome.

On Moshe's wife Sara's fiftieth birthday, the Deichmans hosted a large gathering in their home in the wealthy Glasgow suburb of Giffnock. Giffnock's lush, tree lined avenues were flanked by some of the largest houses I'd ever seen, interspersed with chi-chi boutiques and specialist shops.

I was already familiar with Mark's Kosher Deli as – on special occasions – Moshe would fetch hampers of kosher goodies for the staff – tiny pastrami on rye and reuben sandwiches, matzo ball soup, mini bagels and lox, gefilte fish balls and latkes.

Moshe and Sara's home was unlike anything I'd seen. It consisted of three large interconnected white boxes set back from one another. Each had a flat roof with a grass covering and vast expanses of glass. The interior was a tranquil temple – all soft lighting, white walls and the occasional painting or artefact. Sara was an interior designer and I pondered just how you might go about 'designing' an interior that was virtually empty.

Mark's Deli showed up with the catering and they set up a temporary bar in the echoing entrance hallway. I scanned the gantries for something familiar and left clutching the only thing I recognised – a frothy glass of Warninks Advocaat and lemonade, a glacé cherry balancing precariously on the polished crystal edge.

Sipping my Snowball, I perched on the edge of a cantilevered chrome chair slung through with Zebra hide and set myself up for some serious people-watching. I was soon joined by two quite beautiful young men whom I guessed were two, maybe three years older than me. Honeyed skin and huge spaniel eyes were topped with dark glossy curls. They reminded me a little of Wilson's striking swarthiness, although Gabe and Noah's looks were due to origins I later learned were 'Semitic'.

We laughed and we talked and it soon became apparent that the boys were competing for my attention. I was flattered, but I did wonder if my own dark hair and Old Testament name might be misleading them.

Ah. There was a test I remembered from my childhood.

I turned to Gabe.

"You look kind of familiar. Did you by any chance go to Craigie Park school?"

"Sorry? You went to Craigie Park?"

They exchanged a worried glance then slowly and politely withdrew.

Natan appeared at my side, laughing.

"*Oy **Vey*** Debs! You could have waited before you broke their little hearts! Their Jewish mamas will cut off their newly dropped balls if they even think of dating a *Shiksa*. Bless them - they actually thought they'd discovered some new blood!!!"

Another of my tasks at the Sentinel was to man the eight line switchboard. Two lines would have sufficed normally, as traffic was generally light.

One morning however, I unlocked the front door to discover the switchboard lit up like a fairground ride, all eight lines flashing frantically.

I flicked the first switch.

"**Goood** morning Jewish Sentinel, Deborah speaking."

I was totally unprepared for what followed as I flicked switch after switch, answering line after line.

"You must be very proud of your people."

"You guys did the **impossible**."

"A **thousand** Mazel Tovs."

"What incredible *chutzpah!*"

A torrent of words like plucky, groundbreaking, breathtaking, bravery, unbelievable and unprecedented followed.

I was entirely baffled.

Natan burst through the door, breathless with excitement.

"Debs, have you heard? It's just....it's just.....**incredible**!"

What he was referring to, of course, was the Entebbe Rescue. A wildly daring counter-terrorist hostage rescue had been mounted by commandos of the Israel Defence Forces at Entebbe Airport in Uganda. Two members of the Popular Front for the Liberation of Palestine had hijacked an Airbus A300 with 248 passengers originating in Tel Aviv and were demanding the freeing of a total of 53 Palestinian prisoners.

The hijackers separated out and detained Israeli and non-Israeli Jewish passengers, releasing the rest. Ninety four mainly Israeli passengers along with the 12 member aircrew remained as hostages and were threatened with death.

The rescue operation took place in the night. Israeli transport planes carried 100 commandos to Uganda and in just 90 minutes, of the 106 remaining hostages, 103 were rescued and three were killed. All the hijackers and forty five Ugandan soldiers were killed and eleven Soviet-built MiG-17's and Mig-21's of the Ugandan Air Force were destroyed.

The world community cheered this act of defiant heroism, one of so many throughout Judaism's history.

The Sentinel regularly ran a column celebrating the history of Jewish valour, formulated over two thousand years of exile - not for older readers, but to remind the youngsters coming through of the history that distinguished them and what bound them to one another.

Theirs was the heroism of survival and endurance in often horrific conditions. Persecuted and crushed underfoot, they would rise again and again.

The Jewish festival of Chanukah celebrates a time over two thousand years ago when a small, but determined group of Jews called the Maccabees fought against their Greek overlords to allow Jews to practice their religion freely.

The Greek king had banned all Jewish rituals and tried to force Jews to pray to Greek gods and bow down in front of a statue of the king that had been placed in the Jewish temple. The Jews refused and the Maccabees waged a three year war to regain control of their temple.

The Jews had risen again during the Crusades, the Spanish expulsion, the Russian Pogroms and the Holocaust, maintaining unity, faith and hope, dreaming of the Promised Land where they might be persecuted no more.

It's true that I did feel intensely proud of 'my people'. I was in awe of their resilience, their unity, their wry, raw humour and life-affirming *chutzpah*. I experienced the most visceral of longings to join this brave and exotic community.

Now I know what you're thinking. Who-aaah young Debs. Don't they worship that same God you put yourself on the line for last time? And do you remember how that ended?

If you **had** told me, I wasn't in the mood to listen.

I had to consult.

"Ellen! How do I become a Jew?"

Ellen burst into great peals of laughter.

I was hurt.

When her breathing returned to normal, Ellen wiped her eyes and ruffled my hair.

"Right. Well. First you have to study Jewish theology, rituals, history, culture and customs. You then have incorporate all aspects of Jewish practice into your home life. Some rabbis like you to take one-to-one lessons with them for several months. Oh and you'll probably have to learn Hebrew."

"Okay Ellen. I think I could manage all of that."

Ellen raised an eyebrow.

"Well, that's great. And I hate to be the bearer of bad news. But none of that actually works."

"What do you mean?"

"There's the whole history thing. Thousands of years of expulsions and persecutions, the uprisings, the number of times they've fought back ... that whole shared lineage."

"Ex-actly. It's all of that that excites me and makes me want to join."

"Sorry hon. Doesn't work like that. It's not that anyone ever actually **says** anything. These are nice people. But you know when you don't belong. After all the studying and serious adjustments to my thoughts, my habits and home life, I still don't feel like a real Jew. You can't just acquire their history. To be part of this group you need to be part of the lineage.

Everyone assumes it's about the religion. And to some extent you can convert. But religion's only part of it. And in many ways it's not about that at all. Did you know that more than forty percent of the Jews who live in Israel are atheists? And yet they are still accepted as and refer to themselves as Jews.

Seems to me Debs, that Jewishness can't be just about religion. Jewishness is about race. Race and a long shared history. You can't just acquire that. You can't 'become' Jewish. You are born Jewish."

I was crestfallen. Sure, I knew about the whole shared history thing. I had one. The Catholic-hating one.

I wanted a different one.

Alas, after twenty two fascinating and enjoyable months, Leo and I received our redundancy notices and a basket of goodies from Mark's Kosher Deli.

My job was phased out because the Sentinel's circulation was steadily dwindling and Leo because the old linotype machine was being replaced by computer typesetting.

Oy vey iz mir.

◆ ◆ ◆

In the sad weeks after I departed the Sentinel, I had a dream that would recur with disturbing regularity.

I was alone in a small boat, adrift on a vast ocean. There were many islands in the ocean and on each island were tight little communities, fully engaged in head and heart, smugly confident in the fullness of their belonging.

I would drift on the waves toward each island in turn. I would stretch out my arms and - for just the briefest of seconds - sense rescue. Then the waves would carry me back out to sea.

CHAPTER 6 - LEGS LIKE PELE

My would-be tribe sadly missed (not pissed), I joined the raggle-taggle column of unemployed at the local Job Centre.

The stench of hopelessness clung to the grimy, screwed-down bucket chairs and the worn, stained carpets. In a corner behind a glass screen with a sign that said 'Careers Guidance' was a face I recognised. Mr. Garry. I made an appointment at Reception.

Mr. Garry brightened when he saw me.

"**Deborah!** - How goes it at the Sentinel?"

I explained my new predicament and he nodded sagely before chancing his arm:

"Have you ever thought of university?"

I was more than slightly taken aback. No-one I knew or was related to had even thought of such a thing.

"Erm....not for me. I can't afford it. And besides, you need qualifications."

"Neither of which are a problem" smiled Mr. Garry.

He explained that I was eligible for something called a bursary. That would cover both my fees and a small living allowance to attend South Side Community College where I could study sufficient Highers to apply for a degree course. Thereafter, I could apply for a full student grant which would cover all my university fees for up to four years plus a fairly decent living allowance.

Wow. I was shocked. My tribe's entrenched legend was that university was a privilege reserved exclusively for the bastard toffs.

We agreed that Modern Studies, English and Geography would best support a future in journalism, together with a couple of RSA courses in Pitman 2000 Shorthand and touch typing.

It was a daunting thought. Quite terrifying in its own way. But – being realistic – I was unemployed and Mr. Garry had said that I'd be more or less paid to do it. Since I could offer no justifiable reason to not to at least give it a go, I agreed. And so my future course was set.

❖ ❖ ❖

My classes at South Side took place in a draughty sixties extension to the main Victorian building. My classmates were a mixed bunch. Some nervous looking mature students returning to education after being made redundant or raising children; some like me returning to education after a brief spell away; and others who conversed in a variety of languages that weren't English.

We were joined in the canteen throughout the day by boisterous apprentice hairdressers, brickies, sparkies, and chippies making the most of their day release.

The atmosphere was light, the work interesting and manageable. I was able to condense my classes into three days a week, leaving time for a part-time waitressing job and a bar job. Mam expected me to contribute to my board and lodgings.

At four o'clock on Fridays, some of the teachers would join us in the bar of the hotel at the bottom of the road. When she had time off from her acting course at the Manchester Metropolitan School of Theatre, Caz would join us too.

It was in my Modern Studies class that I met Estelle. Estelle was what Americans call 'preppy'. She travelled each day from the wealthy Glasgow suburb of Newton Mearns (called 'The Merns' by its well-heeled residents and 'Newton Mortgage' by the rest of us). The Mearns was located slap bang in what we Glaswegians called 'The Spam Belt' being that those who bought houses there had so little money left over that they had to live on Spam. Estelle's father was a High Court Judge and stepmother number two a trainee lawyer scarcely older than Estelle.

Like most of my friends, I queued up for my disposable fashion at the famous pile 'em high sell 'em cheap emporium of What Every Woman Wants in Argyle Street – known locally as What Every's, Whatties or Wa Wa's. With our purchases scrunched up and lobbed into those iconic purple and white bags emblazoned with 'What Every Woman Wants', we'd run the gauntlet of cat-calling, hip-thrusting construction workers:

"Come ower here, hen. **I'll** show you what every wummin wants!"

For sure, the fabric was inevitably the cheapest polyester, threads were loose and seams were rarely straight, but we could always get something new to strut our stuff at Glasgow's many night clubs. So what if the average top barely survived a couple of washes? We were hardly looking for long term sartorial returns.

Estelle, on the other hand, invested in her wardrobe. Cashmere cardi's were carefully laundered and regularly de-pilled. Capri slacks were starched and pressed and her beige Russell and Bromley patent pumps shone from judicious application of the appropriate proprietary anti-stain cream. She carried her books in an Etienne Aigner satchel which her great aunt brought back from a trip to New York and while most of the rest of us caught the bus, Estelle drove a bespoke pink Mini Cooper with heart shaped velvet cushions perched on the back window.

I remember clearly the events that led up to Estelle's adopting me as her pet project.

In a Modern Studies lesson exploring relative areas of economic and social breakdown, our teacher had put up a slide of what he referred to as 'The Worst Housing Estate in Europe'.

Excited, I nudged Estelle who was in the seat next to me.

"That's the street I live in! Look, that's our house, top left side of the photo!"

Estelle glared at me, pursing her lips in clear disapproval.

"That's not nice Debsy. You should never joke about such things."

"I'm not joking. It's **true**."

Estelle eyed me with even greater disapproval, opened her pink lipsticked mouth to reply, then thought better of it.

Later, over dishwater coffee in the college canteen, she challenged me.

"You could pass you know."

"Huh? Pass? Pass at what?"

She coloured slightly.

"You know what I mean. You don't **need** to tell people where you come from."

"Sorry? Why would I not? What difference does it make? Where you're born is where you're born. It just is what it is."

Estelle rolled her eyes.

"I can't believe how **naïve** you can be Debsy if you really think it doesn't matter."

Ouch! That stung.

'Naïve' was an accusation Mam threw at me often. I knew Mam's childhood had been a loveless one and it seemed she couldn't bear that anyone else should have better. And as if life weren't cruel enough, fate burdened her with a daughter she couldn't relate to. A daughter her eyes accused of judging her. Ironic that - given Mam invested much of her time in observing and judging everyone else.

I knew from an early age what I was. An idealist in search of a home. Mam saw herself as a realist. Glass not even half full. No glass at all. Hope simply not worth the risk.

She managed a level of accommodation with Davey and Roddy, but not me. I was the accusation. I was the affront.

◆ ◆ ◆

When Caz was home we'd have a few Cider and Babychams at the Griffin (or Spider and Shadybams depending on how many we'd had) and head out to Clouds nightclub which was perched on top of the Apollo on Renfrew Street.

Entry cost 80p and a slightly whiffy lift zipped packed in, well-oiled revellers to the top of the building. Excited, opportunistic boys grasped at the flesh of girls' arses through tightly stretched satin and received a good natured thwack in return.

The resident DJ was Billy Bob Baskin who regularly rolled out a rollicking set dressed in a matted monkey suit.

Clouds was frequented by wannabee hippies and punks, or slick, Bryan Ferry lookalikes. When famous bands played the Apollo, the after gig parties tended to take place upstairs at Clouds. It was totally the place to be seen.

I have hazy memories of one evening when I accidentally slopped my Shadybam over an uber-chiselled guy in a tight, lycra jumpsuit. I apologised profusely and he dried himself off with a bar towel, smiled and asked me to dance with him. At least I think that's what was intended when he introduced himself as Tony Caprioli, took my hand and led me toward the dance floor.

"Ah don't usually hang out with fat girls but Ah like the way you speak. So polite-like."

Caz's jaw dropped. I was all of seven and a half stone.

Apropos of not a lot, Tony explained he was a runner up in Scotland's recent Disco Dance Championships before kicking off a well-rehearsed floor routine. As he spun, I noticed 'Caprioli' spelled out in sequins on the reverse of his suit.

He caught me looking.

"My granny sews them for me." he breathed heavily. "She's very proud."

Once the second chorus of the track came round, the space between us had widened to around seven foot and the crowds on the dance floor were retreating back in noisy annoyance.

"Twat."

"Show off."

"Ravin' poofda."

Giggling, Caz pushed her way through the throng, grabbed me by the hand and pulled me out to the cool air of the foyer. We laughed ourselves hoarse.

"**Sequins**!!"

"His **granny**!!"

"So tight you could tell what **religion** he is."

I thought Estelle could do with some lubricating and loosening up, so I invited her to join us at Clouds next time Caz was up in Glasgow. Her look of distaste said it all.

"Not really my thing sweetie. But I do like a bop. We have discos once a month at my ski club. Why don't you come? You could meet my crowd. They're great fun!"

I declined on a number of occasions, but Estelle insisted. Eventually I broke and agreed to give it a go. On reflection, I think she had someone in mind for her favourite charity case. A suitable boy with a suitable pedigree.

The Moriarty Suite at Estelle's ski club was a brown and beige space, bland and lacking in atmosphere. The boys in Estelle's 'crowd' were amenable in that manner of minor Tory politicians – all hearty back-slapping and haw-haw-haw. The girls were shiny, perjink and inoffensive.

And of course I didn't. Pass, I mean. Sorry Estelle.

They virtually sniffed the air as I was introduced. While they didn't exactly leap backwards, genuflecting and shouting 'Vaccinated 5:10", there was a polite, but discernible shuffling, as if to close ranks and protect the vulnerable.

But – I hear you say, for we're all pop psychologists now – could it be that you transmitted your status to their sub-conscious?

Perhaps I did. But I guess I didn't care not to. I didn't want to join this tribe. I wanted to be a plucky Jew.

◆ ◆ ◆

In the early 80's, Clouds became 'The Penthouse' and then reinvented itself as a roller disco. With the skills I'd mastered at Butlins, I took to rollering with gusto, sketching out zippy figures of eight and skidding backwards around the dance floor.

Ironically, I felt forced to invest in a lycra jumpsuit like Tony's (*sans* sequins of course) for wild-eyed, careering roller-novices would snatch at any loose clothing, pulling my sweaters out of shape and taking me down with them. After multiple bruisings and a few ruined jumpers, I worked out they couldn't so easily grab a handful of lycra.

I remember re-emerging into the cool air at street level after a particularly vigorous and sweaty session to be greeted by a snottery little boy holding the hand of his mother:

"**Mammy**! That lassie's goat legs like Pele."

'Mammy' shot me an apologetic glance.

I grimaced, feeling the need to explain. I pointed at my feet.

"It's the skates. They're…um…heavy."

◆ ◆ ◆

I wasn't at home much that year, so the full revelation of what Davey had progressed to came as a shock.

Davey, Shuggy Lomas, Arthur 'Tart' Higgins and Bobby 'Bobblehead' Marsh had apparently formed a gang called the Hombres. The membership numbers were fluid, but these four were the lynchpins. These four were feared.

They stole from shops and burgled homes. They broke into cars and, roaring drunk on Carlsberg Special, Buckfast and Lannie, would rip round the estate, the waft of burning rubber trailing in their wake. It was when they crashed a stolen Ford Capri into the side of the brick factory on Albion Street that charges were finally pressed.

When it went to court, our family's social worker Brenda (yes, we now had our own social worker) gave an impassioned defence:

"Young David here is a product of a demonised underclass. He's trapped in a ghetto, a hell hole of poor health and grinding poverty. A hell hole characterised by a lack of opportunity, of positive role models and openings for education or advancement. In a situation where such young men are stigmatised, disrespected and labelled as undeserving, is it any wonder that they suffer from a lack of aspiration, from general depression and anomie? Is it any wonder that they fall back on crime and anti-social behaviour?"

Margie, our School Counsellor and Welfare Liaison Officer, rolled her eyes:

"I've known this lad since he was five years old. In my opinion, he's showing clear signs of an Antisocial Personality Disorder. He shows no remorse for the pain he causes, no regard for right or wrong and he is entirely indifferent to the feelings of others. He is violent, manipulative and aggressive."

The judge agreed with Margie and ordered Davey to seek psychiatric treatment.

"**Fuck off**" yelled Davey. "Ah'm no seein' no shrink."

The choice being shrink or custodial sentence, Davey eventually agreed to visit the psychiatrist.

Since Davey refused to do more than grunt at the sessions, Mam and Da were asked to attend on their own to 'provide some background.'

When they returned, Mam, tight-lipped and white-faced, put on her coat and hat, clasped her handbag shut and headed off to the bingo.

Da slumped in his chair.

"How did it go Da?" I asked.

He shook his head.

"Och you know, hen. The usual. They always feel they have to pin it on somebody. So many questions. Wis he abused? Wis there a trauma in his early years? Did ye hit him?"

"Ah can't help wondering if I've failed him. If ah've failed you all. Yer Mam didn't want kids. Ah wanted loads. But it doesnae look like ah've been a good father."

"Da, maybe Brenda's right. Maybe it **is** living here that does it. Brenda reckons we're all just broken."

"But...I dunno....don't ye think a kid can just be born bad? The psychiatrist asked yer Mam how did she **feel** when she gave birth. And – ye know yer Mam – not exactly gushing. So he wrote down the cause was 'lack of maternal affection'. But that can't be right because....well because she didn't...she doesn't lo....."

"It's okay Da. I know what you're trying to say and it's okay. She didn't love Roddy and I either, but we turned out alright."

Da nodded.

"Yer Mam was so smart, y'know. When any o' the teachers asked questions, her hand was always up first. She knew all the answers.

When I asked her to dance at the Lodge I couldn't believe it when she said aye, awright. I mean...a girl like **that**, dancin' wi' me? And before I knew it we were courtin'.

And ah know ah should never have put pressure on her to....y'know. But all the lads were and ah didn't think anythin' would happen. Ye don't, do ye? When yer Mam told me she was pregnant, ah knew what had to be done. Ah had to do my duty and stand by her."

"But couldn't you have g..."

"Naw, hen. We didnae do that in those days. I mean, there were women on the estate who said they could do what was necessary. But it was hellish dangerous. Women died. And anyway....decent folks don't do that kind of thing. So ....Davey came along and, to be honest, that wean was murder from the get go. He cried all the time, he wouldn't feed and when he started to walk and talk he was just so...**defiant**. Everything set him off. Yer Mam became....well, she started to become like she is now."

"But you had other kids?"

Da reddened and looked at the floor.

"Yer Mam also understood about duty. Look, I'm not proud of any of this Debs. It's just how it was then. But when you were born....oh my. You were such a good wean. Always smilin', hardly ever cryin'. I thought maybe yer Mam might change. Back to how she used to be, ken? But if anything she got worse. I dunno. Maybe she was too scared to risk lovin'. Or hopin'. Or maybe she'd just had enough."

"Debs, If I've never said I'm proud of you and Roddy, I want you to know that it's not that I'm not. Because I am."

I gulped, tears pricking my eyelids. I went towards Da, arms outstretched. He pulled away. Maybe it was all just too much for him.

The 'treatment' sessions had no effect on Davey. Emboldened, the Hombres terrorised the estate. Glasgow, then referred to as

Scotland's Murder Capital ,was awash with rival gangs and the Hombres took to carrying cricket bats, knives, swords, hatchets, machetes, bricks and bottles – not it seems for the thrill of anticipated violence, but to protect their territory and their profit.

They graduated from petty theft and joy-riding to much more lucrative organised crime, the perfect vehicle for Davey with his lethal combination of brutality and brains to rise to overlord status.

In a bid to drive down high levels of employment and decrease crime on the estate, the government had given just under £80,000 to local community organisations to underwrite free commercial premises and organise preferential contracts for any businesses set up by local people.

The Hombres, it seems, quickly took advantage of naïve and weak community leaders and gained control of that seed capital. Before long they were indeed employing the local people – that is, the estate's youngsters - to peddle heroin and extort protection money. The gang lent money at exorbitant rates and exacted violent revenge on those who couldn't pay back their loans. No-one on the estate dared grass them.

The police did what they could. They patrolled the estate with whatever manpower they could spare, but when it proved impossible to keep on top of the Hombres' movements, they put several officers and their families in empty council flats in a bid to integrate supervision and gain intelligence on local crime. That didn't work. The officers' homes were set upon week after week, windows smashed, petrol bombs lobbed through letterboxes, the officers' children threatened.

In the end the police families were withdrawn and the Hombres were further emboldened.

Inevitably, flying high on a concoction of heroin and amphetamines, Davey went too far, attacking the leader of a rival gang with a machete. The victim died after three days in intensive care. It was accepted that Davey hadn't actually intended to kill, so he was tried for the lesser charge of manslaughter.

Brenda had reassured Mam that the sentence would be reduced

given Davey's age and background, but the judge thought otherwise and handed down a life sentence in the notorious Barlinnie Prison.

I picture him there, slopping out with the worst excuses for humanity that Scotland has to offer. Who knows, with uncharacteristic good behaviour he could well be out, swaggering amongst us. But we haven't heard from him since his incarceration and we, his family, haven't fallen over ourselves to enquire.

One thing Davey did do for me – and credit where it's due - was to ease my path to discarding the distinctive Glaswegian 'glottal' stop. Whereas I had imagined that it was my friendship with Mhairead that caused the bullies to back off from me, in fact, it was the other way around. It would appear that when one's brother is the feared Lord of the Hombres, one can – with abandon - affect whatever pronunciation one desires.

CHAPTER 7 - CORNUCOPIA

University was what Caz would declare 'a total trip'. A head-spinning revelation.

Buzzing students swarmed from all over the UK and overseas, standing in chattering lines to register for what seemed to me multiple variations of dozens of academic undergraduate and postgraduate topics. So many 'ologies, 'istries and 'isms.

In Freshers' Week it seemed that every one of the 327 student societies had set up their stalls in the Science Hall. Enthused representatives of every academic discipline and sub-discipline co-existed with a cornucopia of leisure and charity groups in cheery harmony.

Leisure offerings included an a capella choir; life drawing; art appreciation; musical theatre; dance; drag; stand-up comedy; opera; jazz; juggling; Shakespeare appreciation; Latin American dance; ceilidh; Gaelic singing; documentary making; creative writing; literature; screenwriting; and something called the Fred Quimby Society (or Freds) which consisted of watching old re-runs of Tom and Jerry cartoons. Allegedly.

Charity groups existed for exiled Palestinians; worldwide refugees; war victims; pacifists; animal rights; gay rights; pro-life; pro-choice; Amnesty; several environmental groups; a food co-op; and two angry competing Feminist groups.

I emerged from the frenetic hubbub of the Fresher's Week market clutching membership applications for one of the walking societies, Hatha yoga, English literature and the name of a coach who – in exchange for the prospect of fondling my arse - would apparently guarantee me a place on the womens' roller hockey team.

I'd taken a deep breath and informed Mam that I'd be moving into one of the on-campus halls of residence. There was little resistance. I guess she must have seen it coming. And besides, Roddy was working now and Davey was out of the house, so one less mouth to feed.

Our halls consisted of two full size, four storey Victorian townhouses in a grand terrace. The buildings had apparently been donated by a distinguished peer in memory of two sons who had graduated from the university then lost their lives in the First World War.

The elaborate, stained glass frontage opened on to a vast hallway with glorious, intact Minton floor tiles and sweeping corbelled archways guarded by plump, heavy-lidded, plaster cherubs, heads resting on chubby forearms. Lofty, coffered ceilings were edged with exquisitely detailed cornices and friezes – egg and dart, dentil, swagged, swan neck and grape vine.

Immediately beyond the imposing reception hall, the decadent grandeur screeched to a halt. All other rooms and common areas had been stripped of original features and replaced with dull, utilitarian linoleum, faded plastic seating, chipped formica tables, strip lighting and cheap 70's Hygena kitchen units. Student-proofed.

Each floor had six twin, shared bedrooms and two highly coveted single rooms. Our large shared kitchen had two temperamental ovens, three scratched hobs and two oversized, noisy fridge freezers.

Floors were alternated – boys and girls. Whatever prim separation was envisioned, it failed to materialise. Boys hid under girls' beds to watch them change or took naked Polaroids of us over the tops of the shared girls' shower cubicles. The rapscallions upstairs stole the special food we prepared for one another's birthdays, adding insult to deliberate injury by returning the dirty dishes and Tupperware to our kitchen. To be washed and no doubt refilled.

We took turns to guard the communal laundry room as our

underwear routinely went missing. Rumour had it that Conor, a shy looking freckly faced lad from Cork, was advertising 'used' knickers and mailing them with the stolen shower photos.

I shared a room with a quiet girl from Dumfries called Lucy. Where I was messy, Lucy was meticulous. Her side of the room was precisely ordered, bed perfectly made, surfaces dusted daily.

Lucy was, in many regards, the ideal room-mate. She didn't play music, watch TV or bring friends or boys to the room. She studied in the library, she slept in her bed, and the rest of the time she was away. I learned only from the other girls that she was an active youth member in the UK Communist Party and when she travelled it was generally to nationwide conferences or – once or twice a year – to Moscow.

Cooking in our shared kitchen was a rumbunctious, highly sociable experience. We exchanged simple, manageable recipes with Greta and Frida – German post graduate medics - and Leike and Veerle, Dutch post-graduate vet students, enthusiastically embracing any tips on how to stretch our meagre allowances to allow for the odd bottle of Blue Nun or a sticky Black Forest Gateau. I learned how to make the cheap, tasteless gravel that was textured vegetable protein earn its keep in just-about-edible lasagnes, chillis and bolognese.

Fong and Sying, Hong Kong Chinese Economics students from two floors below would often come and cook with us, though we discreetly turned our faces and noses away from simmering pans of knuckles, trotters and chicken feet.

Lucy generally hovered on the periphery of these noisy gatherings. She ate little, said little and was – if I'm honest – easy to ignore.

Our campus was straining at the seams with pseudo-Marxists sporting Lenin-look glasses, stained, crispy great coats and regulation army boots. They talked the talk, marched the marches and littered campus with strident, doom-laden leaflets. They seemed, for the most part, entirely insincere and very annoying. Lucy was different. She made no attempt to proselytise or recruit.

As a group we became increasingly curious about what Lucy did when she was away, but I guess we were waiting for her to voluntarily contribute to our lively late-night discussions.

Impatient, Fong decided to mount a challenge.

"Luc-**eee**. Why you go to Mos-cow?"

Lucy sighed, her expression redolent of Stilke's painting of Joan of Arc at the stake. She'd been here before.

Lucy raised her chin. Calmly and evenly, she articulated what she'd clearly explained a number of times.

"I'm a member of the Communist Party. I go there to learn."

"What you learn **there** that is good?"

"Well...instead of wealth and power being concentrated in the hands of a small number, we – our Party - believe it should be returned to its rightful place – with the majority. The people should own the means of their own production and everyone be paid according to need, not greed. If the people control the means of production, then no-one can make and accumulate more money than anyone else.

If we had that here, our system would be fairer. There would be no poverty. Everyone would have the same education, the same status and the same life chances."

Lucy raised her eyes Heavenward and waited. I recognised that look.

"If system so perfect, why everyone in Russia and in China want to leave? Why they are imprisoned or killed if they don't agree?"

"In this country" said Lucy quietly "Our current social and legal system is supposedly in the best interests of the majority. And people who don't conform are labelled anti-social and – yes – often imprisoned. I don't hear objections to that."

"Not the **same**. And anyway, Russian and Communist leaders better capitalists than here. The people have no right to own what they make. It's like...it's like **slavery**.

Mao said "the rulers ideas are the ruling ideas". He meant from before. But now ... **every** idea come from Mao. If you don't agree, you go to labour camp or you die. The people are just what you call.....**widgets.** If they don't behave like good widget and work for the Communist money-making machine they locked away or eliminated.

Chinese can choose nothing for themselves. Not education, religion or what job they do. In Marxist utopia they say everyone will be happy share property and wealth. But the people don't **see** property or wealth to agree to share.

The Communist leaders keep everything. They have all the wealth and all the power. Mao gone but new leader…not good either. Still keeping all the money, all the power.

Capitalism we have in Hong Kong so much better. People have say. So much more free.

You crazy to go Moscow Lucy. Maybe one day they don't let you out."

Veerle, one of the Dutch vet students, placed a gentle, restraining hand on Fong's shoulder. Enough.

Despite the scorching heat of Fong's accusations, it was clear to all of us that the flames did not touch Lucy. Her blissful certainty, her unshakeable conviction remained intact. Did the fact that mere humans seemed unable to apply her political and spiritual ideals invalidate them? She didn't seem to think so.

I remembered where I'd seen that look of transcendence. Wilson wore the same. I'd failed to see the all-too-obvious connection between the two.

A documentary I'd watched a few months previously implied the most fundamental of associations.

Entitled 'Was Jesus the First Communist?" the narrator claimed that any genuine, undefiled grasp of the teachings of Christ compelled followers to support communism as the ideal social system. There was - he claimed - no acceptable alternative.

The narrator suggested that the first Christians, the Apostles included, had practised a type of communism or religious socialism and that the earliest followers of the Christian church had reinforced and perpetuated Christ's political and religious ideals.

However, the leaders of the expanding Church had, over hundreds of years, so distorted Jesus' teachings as to entirely alter the core message and ally Christianity more easily to both the feudal and capitalist systems, which exploited the poor and concentrated wealth in the hands of Church leaders.

The Church had carefully excised from Jesus' teachings the inherent call to action, the exhortation to actually bring about the social justice he referred to as 'The Kingdom of God'. The Church had replaced it with a passive observance that did not call out or threaten the concentration of power.

When the narrator laid out the basic tenets of Christ's teachings and mapped them onto the basic tenets of communist ideology, there did indeed seem to be a compelling area of overlap.

I wondered what Bridie would have made of a dark-skinned Jesus wearing a Che Guevara cap?

And…..- smiling to myself - I wondered what she'd make of a Chinese Jesus?

One wet afternoon when I was around eleven or twelve, I'd come upon Pippy in the comfy seating area of the library. Pencil and front lock of hair behind her ear, she was flicking through a large, glossy book of paintings entitled 'Depictions of Christ in Many Cultures'. She patted the seat next to her.

Delicately rendered in so many exquisite paintings, were all the familiar characters of the New Testament – Mary, Joseph, Christ himself, the Wise Men, the Shepherds, the Apostles, the Angels, the Women at the Well…. the full cast. Except in the first section of the book, every scene depicted only Chinese people. In the next section they had the dark, flat features of many South Americans. And in the following sections they were Korean, black African and North Asian.

"Not the sort of book you'd expect to find in a wee local library, eh?" Said Pippy. "When I saw the title in the catalogue I was intrigued. So I ordered it on temporary loan. Really makes you think, eh?"

I nodded.

"But why would they do that Pippy? I mean, suggest that Jesus and his Mother were Chinese or African? He was Jewish."

Pippy shrugged.

"I dunno. Maybe it's to emphasise that Jesus came to save all races, not just the Europeans. Or maybe they were responding to the Bible's claim that God made man in his image. If you're Chinese, I guess you might interpret that as God would look Chinese. And if you think about it, we in the West have often painted Jesus as light haired, blue eyed and white skinned. That's pretty much the same thing, yeah?"

CHAPTER 8 – MANY PATHS UP THE SAME MOUNTAIN

It was toward the end of my second term of study that I met the man who would dramatically challenge my thinking about life.

I was laying low in the little room we called 'the library' as we – the non-German girls – had offended Greta and Frida who came upon us in the first floor Common Room when we were watching Mel Brooks' Springtime for Hitler'.

"How is it you can **laugh** at this?" they'd raged, eyes filling with indignant tears.

We hung our collective heads, suitably chastened.

The 'library' consisted of a few threadbare armchairs, stained wooden side tables and some tarnished reading lamps. Residents, former and current, had left random piles of tatty fiction and non-fiction books for sharing. Many of the science and economic books were a few years out of date so useful only for reference. The rest were a welcome resource for those of us with little spare cash.

It was there I'd come across a well-handled copy of Ayn Rand's 'The Fountainhead'. The jacket blurb drew my attention. The headline screamed:

"Worldwide Best Seller. More than 6.5 million copies sold and translated into 20 languages. Now a major motion picture."

I flipped it over and read the back cover:

"Howard Roark is an individualist young architect who refuses to compromise with an architectural establishment unwilling to accept innovation. Roark embodies what Rand believed to be the ideal man and his struggle reflects Rand's belief that individualism is superior to collectivism".

Oooh. **Collectivism**. That can be another word for communism, right? I was intrigued.

As I struggled to see past the passages which had been scored through with green highlighter, it struck me that a powerful political message was embedded in the story of Howard Roark. Roark was portrayed as a heroic character, his own happiness the acknowledged and accepted moral purpose of his life and productivity his most noble activity. Rand hammered home again and again (through Roark) the message that the only desirable social system was one that fully respects individual rights as embodied exclusively in laissez faire capitalism.

Deeply engrossed, I initially failed to notice a young man enter the room. On hearing a chair scrape back, I looked up. His shirt sleeves were rolled up to reveal strong forearms and hands that – though large – were at the same time delicate. The top two buttons of his shirt were undone and dark, mesmerising tendrils of hair curled over the edge of his collar. An unruly, wavy mop of hair framed a chiselled face with honeyed skin and large, lash-fringed amber eyes.

When my gaze met his, I was aware only of the slow ticking of the wall clock and the flapping of tiny bird's wings in my chest.

His voice interrupted my rapture.

"What do you think of her ideas?" He inclined his head towards the book.

I gulped. "There's some powerful politics buried in there. Really interesting - yeah. Love the architectural references."

"Her philosophy is called Objectivism. Her mentee Leonard Peikoff has written a book which sets out the tenets of her philosophy. I can lend it to you if you like?"

I nodded. I didn't trust myself to speak.

He smiled.

"Hey, the café at the Hub has finally invested in a proper cappuccino machine. Can I buy you one?"

As we shared an umbrella en route to The Hub, he chattered enthusiastically.

"Did you know that the hero of the novel – Howard Roark – is based on the famous American architect Frank Lloyd Wright? Apparently Rand asked him to design a home for her and he refused. Speculation has it that he didn't like her portrayal of Roark and more specifically, he didn't agree with her philosophy."

He told me his name was Adi – short for Advik – and that his mother Nyra was from Goa in Southern India. She and his father Clive were lecturers at Edinburgh University – Nyra in Micro-Economics and Clive in Applied Linguistics. Adi was in the second year of a Philosophy degree and had one of the single rooms on the first floor of our hall.

Once the hammering in my chest had subsided I could trust myself to speak:

"Philosophy? What does that qualify you for?"

He looked surprised at the question and hesitated for a moment. He smiled:

"Nothing in particular really. It's just something I've always been interested in".

This was an unimaginable luxury. The idea that you could study whatever interested you without reference to either its usefulness for a future career or the level of contribution you might make to the home tribe.

"What do you actually study?"

"Well, at the moment we're looking at nineteenth century Existentialist philosophers. They believe a range of different things, but what unites them is the rejection of traditional systematic or academic philosophies."

"Though" – he laughed "Ironically many of them entirely reject the term 'Existentialist', their argument being that if you were to so label a person you would negate them."

I was flattered that he thought I'd understand. I resolved to find out more, but meantime contented myself with enjoying his extraordinary beauty, observing the way he bit his lip slightly when he was thinking.

Thereafter Adi sought me out with dogged persistence.

It's not that I didn't want to spend time with him. Oh lord, **did** I.

But I was thrown into terror and confusion by the effect he had on me. I thought of Bill and the trail of disillusionment and broken hearts he left in his wake.

I watched Adi as he interacted with others. Relaxed, always joking, he engaged, he entertained, he listened, he sympathised. Where his exotic beauty might have put others on the back foot, he overcame that with his warm, inclusive manner.

I watched in particular how women responded to him. Hair twirling, mirroring his movements, leaning in towards him, mouths open as he spoke. I'd read the pop psychology in the women's magazines at the hair salon. I knew for sure what all of that meant.

No, I couldn't take the risk.

Adi wasn't so easily put off. He taped the first spring snowdrops to my bedroom door. He pushed hand-written excerpts from the poetry of Kahlil Gibran under the threshold. He brought boxes of fragrant spiced buns for my housemates and brought late night pizza when he could hear us in the kitchen. At least he stopped short of using a 'possessed' budgie as a lure...

When all else failed, Adi deployed the most powerful weapon in the armoury of a man wooing a woman. The compilation cassette.

Boxed, wrapped and beribboned, I found it outside my door when I returned from the gym.

And – I have to say – the boy chose well.

Side A – You Are So Beautiful; Wonderful Tonight; Sometimes When We Touch; Baby I Love Your Way; You Are the Sunshine of My Life; Could it Be I'm Falling in Love.

Side B – I'd Love You to Want Me; Just The Way You Are; You've Got a Friend; If; When I Need You; The First Time Ever I Saw Your Face.

When resistance became an almost daily trial, I knew I had to consult.

I generally avoided using the payphone on our floor as it was bang in the middle of the landing and all conversations could be heard on that floor and on the stairs of the ones below and above.

But this was an emergency.

The phone rang for some time before a sleepy sounding girl answered.

"Can I speak to Caz please?"

"**Caz**!" she screeched. "Phone for you."

"Caz? How **are** you?"

"**Debs!** Oh you know. The usual. Trying to summon a shit to give. How are you Babes? What's happening?"

"Oooh…I'm not so good."

"What gives?"

It's a guy."

"Uh-**huh**."

"I like him."

"Uh-**huh**."

"It's just….it's like…it's like I'm punching above my weight, you know? Like for sure I'm going to get myself hurt."

"Hey, hey. Come on Debs. Take a chill pill. Tell me about him."

I told her everything and as I did, I felt the rising tide of love for and pride in the man I was describing. Oh, bloody hell!

"Tell you what Babes, why don't I come meet him?"

◆ ◆ ◆

"Wow. Just wow." Caz was impressed.

"I mean . . . " said Caz "the way he **looks** at you. No-one's ever looked at me that way. You've got nothing to worry about girl. Relax. Enjoy. This man's a keeper."

"Yeah Caz, but the way he is with women. How could I ever feel ….. safe?"

Caz dragged me into one of her crazy bear hugs.

"You stupid girl. Watch how he is with other men. And older women. He treats everyone the same. All that's different is how women respond to him and you can't blame him for that. He's crazy about you Debs. Make the most of every gorgeous minute and I'll try not to be tooooo jealous!"

❖ ❖ ❖

Trust established and terror abated, thereafter Adi and I were pretty much inseparable. We spent endless hours sharing ideas and books, squashed together on his narrow bed watching films on the tiny portable TV he'd smuggled into halls.

The progression to love-making was gradual and natural. It was never a thing that was assumed or discussed. It just happened. Softly, respectfully and wonderfully. I loved the person I saw reflected in his eyes. The deep wells of affection, the admiration and – above all – the pure, uncomplicated love.

❖ ❖ ❖

The Easter break was looming and with Adi intent on going home to study for his exams, I realised just how much I would miss him.

"Come home with me for at least a couple of days Debs" Adi pleaded. "Mum and Dad will love you."

Nyra and Clive lived in an echoey main door flat in a Victorian tenement in leafy Morningside, Edinburgh. Where Moshe and Sara's home had been uber-minimal, Nyra and Clive's was uber-maximal.

The grand entrance hall with its stained glass and polished, stripped wood flooring reminded me of Halls. But where all character had been removed beyond the Halls' entrance, the original Victorian features of this home had been carefully and respectfully restored. Cool, white walls formed the perfect backdrop for large gilt-framed mandalas, Clive's many black and white photos of iconic Edinburgh landmarks and his bright, surrealist abstract paintings.

Bright chunky throws adorned two slightly threadbare linen chesterfields and delicate rosewood antiques, balloon back chairs, a small writing desk and some hexagonal based side tables provided platforms for framed photos of extended family on both sides. There were photos of a youthful Nyra and Clive in traditional white wedding attire and an adjacent photo of what I took to be a Hindu marriage ceremony, the couple circling a fire pit wearing large floral headbands. There was Nyra in later years alongside smiling women in vibrant, jewelled saris and Clive with men in gold brocade salwar kameez and elaborate headdresses. A collage of Adi-through-the-years bore witness to his development, toothy baby through to downy lipped teenager.

An intricately carved chessboard sat on a folding table in pride of place. Clive was a chess Grandmaster and, according to Adi, had had little to no success in interesting his only child in the game. It was, Adi told me, at a chess tournament in Kerala that Nyra and Clive had met.

Nyra was – or at least had been - something I had never heard of and struggled to get my head around. She was a chess groupie. It was apparently a thing in India where young players are hot housed in elite chess schools and the best of them are given a level of state backing that allows them to be pretty well-paid full-time chess players. It seems that Grandmasters in India enjoy much the same status and adulation as the West's elite footballers.

A mish-mash of bookcases lined three walls of the sitting room. There were books everywhere – academic, reference, classic, fiction, paperbacks, hardbacks and children's books. One drew my attention – Bertie Bear's Beginners Chess for Children.

"Welcome Deborah."

Nyra, bangles softly jangling, smiled and bid me sit. I could see Adi had inherited her delicate features and large doe eyes.

"Thank you. Everyone calls me Debs."

Adi's parents were as relaxed and charming as he'd described them. They asked lots of questions and listened intently. I felt completely at home and was glad I'd conquered my nerves and agreed to come.

At six foot five, Clive was a large, broad chested bear of a man, yet his movements were gentle, his manner warm and his eyes perpetually smiling. I wondered momentarily what it might be like to climb up onto his fatherly lap and be comforted. My heart was pierced through with an intense shard of longing.

Adi took me upstairs and showed me into a large room with a bay window, a window seat and an enormous swagged bed.

"This is where our honoured guests sleep, puchki."

The following morning I showered and dressed and Adi led me through to the same sitting room I'd sat in the previous evening. A slanted blade of sunlight pierced the early gloom, illuminating the mandalas and showcasing their brilliant shapes and colours.

In one corner, Nyra was quietly poised at the little rosewood desk on which she'd placed a silver tray and some small figurines. On the tray were a small silver bell, what looked like a miniature oil lamp, an incense burner, a pot of water with a tiny spoon and some petals.

The smell of incense reminded me of carefree evenings *chez Caz*.

I drew back, sensing I'd interrupted a private moment.

Nyra beckoned.

"Don't be shy young Debs. Come see. I'm making my morning puja. It's how we Hindus honour the divine and welcome God and special guests into our home."

She smiled benevolently, indicating once again that it was I who was the special guest. I had begun to suspect that I was the only girl Adi had brought to his home.

Nyra proceeded with the ritual, explaining each stage.

"I ring the bell, **see**, to let God know that I've come to worship and inviting him into our home. Then I make circles with the lamp to bring light to my shrine. The light is a symbol of God's presence. The incense stick purifies the air and with this spoon I symbolically offer God water to drink and to wash."

I looked at the little figures.

Nyra guessed what I was thinking.

"Most people think Hindus worship many gods. But that's not quite accurate. We believe there is one universal spirit which we call Brahman. Brahman is everywhere in the universe, including inside every living thing.

God shows himself to human beings in many different forms, both animals and human. These manifestations of gods and goddesses help us to understand and dwell upon the many facets of God."

My eye caught something unexpected in the corner of the makeshift shrine - a small, silver framed picture of the Sacred Heart.

"Ah. You're wondering why I have a picture of Jesus on my shrine? We Hindus have a saying:

'There are many paths up the same mountain'.

History has gifted us many learned teachers and prophets. They all in their own unique ways offer us guidance on the road to enlightenment. But the path is our own. No-one can tell us how to walk it. No-one can walk it for us."

Her morning ritual complete, Nyra headed to the kitchen to prepare our breakfast.

"I'm making idli, Adi's favourite breakfast."

She ruffled his hair affectionately.

Adi explained.

" Idli are a type of steamed savoury pancake made from fermented black lentils and rice. Mum usually serves them with a lentil, vegetable and tamarind stew called sambar."

If I'm honest, it sounded like a dreadful dish to start the day, but I was surprised by how feather light and delicious it was.

In the two days that followed, Nyra served up an extraordinary array of South Indian delights – Masala Dosa stuffed with a spicy mash of potato and onion; Andhra lamb curry; vadas – a type of savoury doughnut; Malabar parotta – a type of flaky flatbread with a chunky beef dish cooked with spices, coconut and chillies; and a spicy Bhatkali biryani. For dessert on the second evening we had a speciality normally reserved for festivals and major events – payasam which is made by adding rice to boiled, sweetened milk and adding cashews, almonds and cardamom.

Alas, Adi had not inherited his mother's cooking skills, though after each trip home he returned with his 'takeaway' – carrier bags containing an assortment of overstuffed Tupperware dishes.

As we left their home, Nyra took both of my hands in hers:

"Daughter, we are so happy that our boy will have such companionship and love on his journey."

She then drew me into a long, maternal embrace that brought on a sudden rush of tears.

◆ ◆ ◆

Driving back to Glasgow in Adi's battered old Datsun, I asked him if Nyra had wanted him to be brought up a Hindu.

"No. Both parents said 'find your own path son'. They didn't direct me or force on me any traditions from either of their upbringings. They encouraged me always to work things out for myself."

"You don't miss being part of an established community with shared values then?"

I was thinking my own attachment to the plucky Jews.

He thought about it for a moment.

"No. Not at all."

I hesitated.

"Can I ask you a question? I'm worried you might be offended."

He smiled.

"Ask away."

"Your mum's religion – it's very beautiful, yeah? Very liberal, very tolerant. It's just that….and I'm not sure how to say this. But the **caste** system…"

"Is repressive and ugly. Doesn't fit? Well spotted Debs. And there's good reason for that.

Historical research shows that it was grafted on to the indigenous Dravidian religion by invading Aryans from modern day Iran. The Aryans were light skinned and as conquerors, were keen to prevent dilution of their blood by that of the dark skinned Dravidians. So they instituted a highly repressive social system designed to keep the Dravidians in their place – that is, as servants to the Aryans.

But – and here's the clever bit – to ensure total observance by the Dravidians, they linked it to religion. It was God's will that they accept their allotted roles in life and for this obedience they were promised a higher caste in the next life. And so the caste system was born."

"So it's basically the tool of a repressive political regime then?"

"Yeah, you could say that. But disguised as a vital component of religion."

"So why do people in India still adhere to it?"

"Well, it's technically illegal now for it's been recognised just how damaging it is to the society. But because of its ingrained religious context, people won't simply turn their backs on it. For someone who believes they've spent multiple lifetimes working their way through what was sold to them as a guaranteed system leading to enlightenment/freedom/nirvana – whatever they choose to call it – how might they simply extract themselves?

What social structure might replace it? What would happen to all the festivals and community rituals that form the backbone of the society, punctuate life and give it meaning?

Even if you take someone as enlightened and intelligent as my mother? She's a Brahmin for a start. She's already at the top of the social stratification. You could say she already has her insurance policy.

No, it's just not that simple. And – as in British society – there's a class element to it all. For example, here you could win the lottery tomorrow, buy a big house in the most fashionable area then punt yourself as upper class. But it doesn't work that way. You would still be – you would always be - 'new money'. And if you reverse it, someone who was born into 'old money' who fell on hard times would nonetheless be seen as aristocratic. You can't just change sides.

I thought about Ellen and her thwarted attempts to 'become' Jewish. I thought about the Feen-yins and the Proddy Dogs. They didn't change sides.

I pondered why it might be that the religion that seems the most reasonable, the most desirable, the 'Only True One' is inevitably the one that is prevalent in the society into which one is born. I knew of only one person who had actually tried to change sides and they would not have her.

Adi was lucky. No-one had offered him sides to take. And yet it seemed to me that we humans do have an inherent drive, a deep seated genetic compulsion to belong. We do, don't we?

CHAPTER 9 - YOU CAN CHOOSE YOUR FRIENDS

After the roaring success of my meeting with his parents, Adi, was all too eager to be introduced to my tribe.

I put him off for as long as I could, then bowed to the inevitable. What would be would be.

I asked Mam if I could bring him for tea, my thinking being that tea wouldn't prolong the agony for longer than was strictly necessary.

There was, of course, only one way this could go. With his extraordinary beauty, his easy manner and his unfailing and genuine interest in details of other peoples' lives, Adi had a reasonable expectation of being adored. He simply wouldn't expect to draw a blank with Mam. Why would he?

Nyra – on hearing of the impending visit – had baked little fragrant spiced buns and placed them in a be-ribboned brocade box with a note that said:

"May my son gladden your hearts as your beautiful daughter has gladdened ours".

Ho boy! Reduced to the size of that small box, were Nyra's towering hopes for a joy-filled union of two families.

Mam said nothing. She simply withdrew the buns and placed them on a plate. Da tried to lighten the atmosphere, but Adi's sheer otherness and the overwhelming tension of the occasion was just too much for him. Da was awkward and tongue-tied. And if he was waiting for a signal from Mam that it was okay to like Adi, it didn't come.

I'm reminded of something Ralph Glasser would later write in his book 'Growing up in the Gorbals':

"...For a Gorbals man to come up to Oxford was as unthinkable as to meet a raw bushman in the St. James club, something for which there were no stock responses. In any case for a member of the boss class, someone from the Gorbals was in effect a bushman, the Gorbals itself as distant and unknowable as the Kalahari Desert."

To my family, Adi might as well have been a bushman. And his golden, loving, privileged family life the Kalahari Desert.

Adi had prepared himself well for the financial poverty I'd described. I daresay he'd seen far worse on family trips to Goa. But where Estelle had demonised my past and bid me reject it, Adi embraced it with such vigour that he sepia-tinted and romanticised it. In the end, neither hit the mark.

What Adi hadn't foreseen and had no resources to deal with, was the deep-rooted, entrenched bitterness; the doggedly narrow world view; the sheer determination to resist all hope; and that furious, utterly intransigent sense of thwarted entitlement. This was, in the purest sense, all that embodied the ethos of my tribe. I wondered just how Adi might romanticise that.

In Roddy, however, Adi found a kindred spirit. They were fast friends instantly and spent many hours drinking Ouzo and discussing just how far removed the Western concept of Buddhism, with it dogged obsession with self, was from that of Eastern Buddhism.

Roddy had had a brief flirtation with Buddhism, but had rejected the idea of reincarnation and what seemed – to him - the implied suggestion that disability, illness or just plain bad luck could be seen as resulting from bad karma in a previous life.

On that first evening I introduced them, when Adi left to top up our drinks, Roddy took my hand in his:

"Adi's everything you deserve Debs. It's great to see you so loved."

◆ ◆ ◆

About six months into my studies, it was dawning on me that the journalist's job was not to simply report The Truth. In our lectures we examined various types of fallacious arguments, not, as I had naively imagined, to call them out, but to better utilise them in future employment.

In a summer placement with our local angry tabloid, I was exposed to what struck me as the most fallacious excuse for journalism.

An ugly, established bias was shoe-horned into every column inch of reporting. That bias was that the 'boss' class and the government were evil, exploitative and not to be trusted and the working classes – on the other hand - were honest, hard-working, innocent, hapless tools to be exploited and gobbled up by their capitalist overseers. It was distorted, dishonest and sensationalist. And – alas - all too familiar, it being the overwhelming theme tune of my childhood.

I ventured once or twice to express my belief that perhaps the readers deserved better. I was quickly shut down and informed that it was their (the working classes') own paper and the one they freely chose to buy. The views routinely expressed in the paper – they said - were simply reflecting the customers' own beliefs and sentiments and were not in any way directed by, or indeed inflamed by, the newspaper.

Lies, lies, damned lies. It troubled me to what degree the newspapers' mostly middle-class reporters parroted the party line and wrote what they could not possibly understand, let alone believe. Observing the burning embers of an issue, they poured lighter fuel on it, the better to exaggerate and perpetuate a skewed, narrow minded perspective that sold newspapers. But that – it seems – is the sad, browbeaten animal that is contemporary commercial journalism.

◆ ◆ ◆

The only other member of Adi's family I met in the early days was his cousin on his father's side.

Sal was what people generously describe as a 'character'. She wore only black, shapeless, linen clothing. Her coats, hats, shoes, bags, folders – everything was black. Her dyed black hair formed two heavy curtains either side of her ashen face. Her simmering, malevolent facial expressions reminded me of Wednesday Addams.

Sal hung out with Adi's friends and they were generally joined by Sal's two flatmates – Eddy and Mags - who were female, but overtly more masculine than the boys. Sal was rude, superior and dismissive. I made the mistake once or twice of bounding up to her with a clearly distasteful amount of enthusiasm:

"**Hi**, Sal how are you doing? What's happening?"

Her stock response? A disdainful glance and a dismissive "Hey."

I asked Adi what the boys thought of Sal.

"Oh they're terrified of her. Well, you would be, wouldn't you?"

"But I guess she's okay when you get to know her?"

Adi grinned.

"No. Not really."

For reasons that I could not discern, Sal gifted me a book.

"Here. You look like the sort of person who should read this."

Ah. Marilyn French's "The Women's Room". Riiiggght. The book had taken the female literary world by storm just a couple of years previously and was an instant best seller, greedily and publicly devoured by legions of angry and embittered women.

And here in this book by Marilyn French were the same obvious and ugly fallacies I'd found so untenable at the tabloid. Not working class versus boss class this time, but men versus women.

The story told of a group of mainly middle class women who struggled with the banal reality of being housewives and mothers, married to men who were violent and selfish bullies.

To me, it had an air of almost comic tragedy. The women, as carefully depicted, were dynamic and heroic, every detail of their lives and personalities drawn in melodramatic detail. The men – clearly set up from the outset as straw men, were mere caricatures. They lacked any real depth, were unsympathetically drawn and were there simply to 'prove' to what degree men made the lives of women miserable.

At one point the narrator (who turns out in the end to be the main character that is, French herself) remarks that there are easy ways to destroy a woman:

"You don't have to rape or kill her; you don't even have to beat her. You can just marry her."

This struck me as woefully wide of the mark. Since when were the complex relationships between men and all women so easily reduced to one polarised dynamic?

Even I, with a fairly limited world view, knew that there were men who were 'feminine'. Men who were gentle. Men who would have loved to be house husbands at a time when such a thing was unheard of. And yes - I knew of women who were ambitious and successful in their own right.

Of course there were – and still are – women who experience physical violence. But violence comes in many forms. I thought of Da. He worked long hours at a boring, thankless factory job to support his family and at the end of each week handed over his meagre wage, receiving in return his 'pocket money' which was basically just enough for a couple of pints.

His rueful term for Mam was 'she who must be obeyed'. Mam articulated his failures as a man at every turn and her acrid disappointment at the lives she might have had and had been denied. This raw, relentless torrent of dissatisfaction was directed mostly at my father and, to his shame and humiliation, freely voiced in company.

Mam got pregnant with Davey before marriage and Da had, as men in those days were societally obliged to do, stepped up and done his duty. I don't recall ever hearing him complain, despite receiving no credit for his unwavering support. But worse than the relentless criticism and the lack of credit was the denial of love from Mam. In any form.

Had he longed for a smile from Mam, an approving look or a soft touch as I had? I don't know. I wish I had asked.

Did he find solace in golden-edged dreams in which Mam bestowed love, tenderness and approval, only to wake to the reality of the tight-lipped bitterness, the cold, clammy touch? I don't know.

But, after a couple of pints of Tennents at the Lodge on a Saturday night, it was as though two severed wires re-connected and the feelings from which he had insulated himself returned. He was softer then, more loving and we, his children, glimpsed the man he could have been.

And the 'mind-numbing boredom' which was how French described housework? That didn't resonate with me either.

The social structure described in French's novel was as alien to me as the Kalahari. The far more complex reality as experienced by my tribe, had – in addition to any number of dissatisfied wives – downtrodden, bullied men and kids who ran homes and were denied the luxury of a childhood.

It struck me that French's novel better described the grinding materialism of upward mobility. More of a cold, emotionless contract between wife and husband than a relationship, the woman's fulfilment sidelined to allow the husband to more freely pursue a career that would bring money and status to him and to his family. That was the deal, their destiny, their culture.

I thought about Estelle. This was more her world. Estelle would marry money, surely?

I tried to imagine Estelle loving the way Adi and I did – the breathless, raw abandonment; the torrents of emotion that took us to the edge then back; the sweet opening up both physically and emotionally. But in my mind I could see only perfunctory kisses, dutiful sex in exchange for a life of comfort and status, albeit repetitive and boring.

I must at this point confess my embarrassment at having so underestimated Estelle. For having been so ready and willing to accept the proffered cliché. Had I known what initiative she would show and what she would do, I would have grabbed her, hugged her and said:

"You go girl."

And as for Sal. Did I share with Sal my considered thoughts on French's fallacious arguments?

Oh yes.

She threw her arms around me and said:
"I just **knew** you'd get it" . . . . .
Only kidding. I returned the book through Adi and hid.

◆ ◆ ◆

Some weeks later Adi and I were leaning cross legged against his bedroom wall listening to Chris Rhea and sipping from small bottles of Strongbow.

Half laughing, half embarrassed, he chose that moment to confess:

"Debs. If I tell you something, will you promise not to share it with anyone?"

I promised.

"Last April Fool's Day I played what I thought would be **the** most brilliant prank on Sal. You know she works as a Production Engineer in the Tennent's Lager Brewery in Dennistoun? . . ."

I knew it well. Depending on the wind direction the pungent, hoppy aroma would waft through the windows of our rooms and make our clothes and hair stink.

. . . ." And you know how Tennents have those photos of scantily clad women on the side of the cans?"

Ah yes. The so-called Lager Lovelies. One of the on-campus Feminist groups had been distributing leaflets calling for those photos to be banned. The leaflet depicted a leery looking old man holding up the can. A speech balloon had him saying to the model:

"Honey. Ah had my hauns roun' you last night."

" Well" – said Adi " I asked Sal's flatmate Eddy to sneak a Tennent's letterhead from Sal's room. We photocopied it then mocked up a fake letter, yeah?"

"Ooh, clever. What did it say?"

"Ah. Here's the good bit. Well, okay it was supposed to be the good bit. It said that Tennents' management had decided, that year, to recruit the 'Lovelies' from inside the company. Sal had been selected and was being invited to come along for a photo-shoot the following day and she was to bring 'suitably loose clothing'."

An image of Wednesday Addams' head on Rachel Welch's voluptuous bikini-clad body entered my head and I spat out my Strongbow. Clutching my innards, I laughed till it hurt.

"Oh my **God** Adi! She must have been livid that anyone thought she would even entertain such a thing!"

"Well **no**. Here's the thing. She apparently ran through to Eddy's bedroom all excited and asked Eddy if she had anything scanty and sexy she could wear."

I cringed. "Oh **no**! And I guess Eddy had to tell her it was all a joke?"

"Yeeeeah. Sal didn't take it well to say the least. She wouldn't talk to me for weeks and when I explained that we hadn't expected her to react like that, it only made things worse.

It caused a huge to-do in our family. Apparently Sal felt totally humiliated. And exposed, I guess. My Mum and Dad were furious and sat me down for a right talking-to."

Adi affected his mother's soft melodic tone:

"Adi, my boy, your dad and I did not raise you to behave in such a cruel way. Especially not to a family member and one who is so sensitive."

"**Sen**-sitive?" I thought of Sal's rudeness, her supercilious manner.

Adi guessed my thinking. He bit the edge of his lip.

"Yeah, she's been cold and unapproachable like that since she was little. I guess she rejected us before we got the chance to reject her."

CHAPTER 10 - THE MONSTER IN THE CUPBOARD

It was an evening that started like so many others.

Adi and I were lying on his bed, my head nestled on his chest, Adi stroking my hair. I was happily recounting my various stories – growing up on the estate, Mhairead, Caz, Erik, Wilson, Estelle and the plucky Jews – when Adi said softly, almost inaudibly:

"You're a funny little thing Debs. Always looking for somewhere to belong. Never really finding a home. Have you ever thought of just belonging to yourself?"

I sat up and scanned his face. It was clear he meant no criticism.

"I don't understand Ads."

"Come. Sit with me."

He propped himself up against the wall and bid me come sit next to him. He took my hand.

"There's something I'd like to explain to you Debs but it's kind of complicated. If you'll bear with me I'll try to make it as easy to understand as I can. But just stop me at any point if you're not following, yeah?"

I nodded.

He took a deep breath.

"**So**...there's this crazy-sounding French philosopher called Jean Paul Sartre. He says – and I have to say I don't like this particular way of putting it – that we're all condemned to be free. What he means is that there is nothing intrinsically in life that gives it meaning. That all searches for meaning are doomed to failure for there is nothing to find."

"Nothing? I have to say you're not selling it to me Adi."

"Patience, puchki. There **are** philosophers – solipsists they're called – who do say that we can't prove there is anything at all in the world outside of our own heads. This isn't that. What Sartre is saying is that humans can and should make individual, rational and conscientious choices about what they believe.

Life, he says, is a perpetual conflict between oppressive, spiritually destructive conformity - that is, sticking doggedly to what we've been taught – and what he calls an authentic, spiritually uplifting and totally liberating way of being.

Sartre talks of experiencing 'nausea' – another term I'm not especially keen on – but what he describes is an everyday life which is tainted with a pervasive, horrible taste. This, taste, he says, is the innate, nagging reminder of our responsibility to grasp true freedom, a subconscious rejection of the norms we've been forced to swallow.

Sartre feels we – most of us - are doing everything we can to avoid taking up that freedom. Yet no matter how much we strive to comfort and distract ourselves with the 'certainties' of tradition, culture, religion, history and beliefs about intrinsic human nature, these are entirely bogus. We can run, but we can't hide.

He says if you refuse to choose each and every belief for yourself, you will be burdened for life with disorientation, confusion and a profound restlessness, A deep spiritual dissatisfaction. Authenticity has to be earned, not learned.

If you will not step up and author your own choices, you will necessarily be burdened by the choices of others. Alas, many - indeed most - he says, are hungry for and grateful to accept other's choices because they are too afraid of the void, the terrifying necessity and responsibility of making their own paths in life. Yet in the deepest levels of their subconscious, is the knowledge that not only are they living a lie, but it's someone else's lie.

These smug 'islands' in your dreams Debs, full of people so certain in their beliefs, united in a common cause? I see them too. But not the way you do. I see islands alright, but the peoples' lives are blighted by fear. They're unfulfilled, wracked by secret doubt and too terrified to take those first steps into the water.

They say Mother Theresa lost her faith in later years. Did she somehow simply lose her beliefs or did she outgrow them? Could it be that, approaching the end of her life, she grasped one last chance to author her own reality?

Whatever is the case, it seems she then drew back from publicly acknowledging a life dedicated to a dogmatic belief system she no longer subscribed to. But why? Why didn't she step up and speak out? How could she continue to not only pay lip service to that which she no longer believed, but to influence and direct the lives of others on the basis of those beliefs?"

I felt giddy. There was something in this, but I didn't like it.

"But Adi, how would anyone **do** what Sartre suggests? Just throw away **everything** they've ever believed to be true and….and be left with what? Without structure, would we all not simply fall into some sort of spiritual abyss or turn to anarchy?"

"I agree, you couldn't just throw everything away at once. But think about it. If every time you had to make an important decision or pass on an opinion to others, you engaged your own logic and creative power to overcome your learned social and moral context in pursuit of new values … and genuine aesthetic health? In the fullness of time your beliefs would become progressively more authentic and – I believe – that feeling you constantly describe of dissatisfaction, of being a fish perpetually out of water would dissipate."

Now I did feel fear. I did feel something akin to a sort of nausea. I felt like a child, believing there's a monster in the cupboard. Compelled to check and check again.

I was on a rickety rope bridge crossing over a chasm. I looked down and I saw the sun glint off the pure clear water below, but between me and the water was the danger of annihilation, the spectre of the unknowable.

Adi stopped for a moment, searching my face for a reaction.

"You following this Debs? You comfortable with what you're hearing?"

I nodded, not yet trusting myself to speak.

Adi continued.

"So….these **islands**, yeah? These people who inhabit closed religious, political, economic and cultural mono-systems? How often does the disjoint between competing systems result in needless grief, conflict and war?"

"Sadly, far too often. But humans are social Adi. We can't live in bubbles of one."

"Indeed. But just say – and bear with me on this one – instead of merely accepting whatever beliefs and traditions we're born into, instead of simply acting the part to keep our place in the tribe or the society, we author our own beliefs **then** seek out others with the same or similar beliefs? They wouldn't have to have a full set of entirely the same beliefs. Just some that would overlap. Like a Venn diagram?

So what I'm seeing in my head, yeah, is each and every person robust, fulfilled and steadfast in their commitment to constantly author and re-author their own belief systems. At various points they will naturally join with others who share complementary elements of their individual beliefs. Like a sort of matrix or reinforced mesh. Can you see how that would lead to a stronger, more solid and more authentic society?

There would be no need to persecute and make war with others. To suck on the stale air of ancient grievances, rehashing old hatreds, focussing cross-eyed on the minutiae of trumped up offence. For the whole concept of unthinking tribal affiliation would have been outgrown. We're intelligent beings. If we wanted to, we could breathe the fresh air of liberation.

And, yeah, I know it sounds idealistic but in a rational society, 'human nature' and 'brute tribalism' can be left behind. And we can rejoice in what binds rather than separates us."

I nodded, my thoughts racing. Adi took both my hands in his and we held one another's gaze.

"I'm so glad I found you Debs."

"And I you"..

◆ ◆ ◆

My head spun and, for days, my thoughts chased one another in relentless circles. I needed to consult.

Caz had a two-for-one pizza coupon for Zesty Pesto on Great Western Road. We'd hardly taken our seats when Caz burst:

"So **Babes**…what's this big revelation Adi's been giving you?"

I took a deep breath.

"Phew. Yeah. Right. Sooo…there's this guy. A famous French philosopher – Jean Paul something. He wrote a book that says there's basically nothing. Not as in no-thing. More that there's no **meaning**. So you shouldn't waste your time going looking for it. You have to make your own meaning."

I glanced over to the couple on the adjacent table. The woman – the better to hear our conversation - was leaning so far towards us that her chair was balancing on the two side legs.

Caz and I grinned at one another and I continued *sotto voce.*

"**And**, if you don't make your own meaning… you'll suffer from something he calls 'nausea' which means you'll never feel comfortable in your own skin. Never settle properly to anything. So you have to decide all the important stuff, like what you believe and how you act by applying your own values, your own logic."

Caz grimaced, crossed her eyes and swung back in her chair.

"Eeeeeesh….!!!"

"Okay, it's all a bit on the heavy side, but do you get the drift?"

"Yeah, Babes I do get what you're saying and Adi makes a very good point. We do, most of us, want to fit in so we tend to keep to the rules. And there are so many rules about how we should live, what we should wear, what's acceptable and what's not, who or what is the right god for us, what's to be valued and what is not, what is moral and what is not, what constitutes success and what does not. We all conform. Why and at what cost?"

"Not you though, Caz."

"Really? Think about it Babes. My clothes, the hair, the taste in music, my over the top personality. Who **am** I?"

I gave it a minute.

"You mean, you think you're **Maureen**?"

"Correct. But you Babes, you've always been yourself."

◆ ◆ ◆

In the days that followed, I was lost in contemplation of both Adi's and Caz's words. I peered into the cupboard's depths again and again to check on the monster; leaning gingerly over the rickety bridge to gaze at the sparkling water below. I tossed and turned in dreams of falling, waking soaked in sweat, weary and confused.

In time, my anxiety subsided and I made my accommodation with the monster that was this strange but exhilarating new perspective. Sleepless nights were gradually replaced with soft, golden-lit dreams where I would fall into a warm and comforting maternal embrace I'd never known.

The giddiness left me and was replaced with an unfamiliar sense of calm, a quiet, spiritual high, the by-product of a gradual coming home. To safe harbour. To myself. I felt strong. Determined. I was on the path to a new, sustainable kind of belonging and I would not be diverted.

Did I mention I was naïve?

CHAPTER 11 - FOR WHOM THE BELLS . . . .

The first derailment came quickly and from the least expected source.

Two or three evenings a week, Adi worked as a waiter at the Chowdhury Club, one of the grander Indian restaurants in Glasgow.

He looked almost comically handsome in his work uniform. It consisted of a red wool jacket with thick black and gold braiding trimming the lapels and the front panels of the bodice; black knee length harem pants; gaiters; spats; and a red and gold brocade turban. The pay wasn't great, but gratuities for Chowdhury's most charming waiter were not inconsiderable.

For my birthday, Adi had booked a coveted window table at the Chowdhury. Dressed in an emerald silk maxi dress I'd borrowed from Leike, I scanned the menu and ordered Prawn Koliwada as a starter and Mattar Paneer for a main course.

Adi had always said the food at the Chowdhury Club wasn't as authentic or as good as his mother's and he was right. But it was pretty damned good.

Adi put down his fork and gazed lovingly across the red-clothed table:

"You look seriously gorgeous tonight Debs. That dress really brings out the colour of your eyes."

This wasn't Adi's usual jokey style. He looked strangely nervous and his voice warbled when he spoke:

"There's something I'd like to ask you."

He swallowed and his Adam's apple bobbed.

"You know I love you yeah? And I loved you from the moment I set eyes on you? Would you do me the honour of becoming my wife?"

He took my hand and placed an exquisitely ornate ring in my palm. It was crafted from white metal and consisted of two delicately detailed feathers entwined in a circlet. Woven into the fronds of the feathers were dozens of tiny precious stones – sapphires, emeralds and rubies.

"It was my grandmother's."

I was speechless.

Adi ploughed on.

"Yeah…I know this has come out of the blue and will be a bit of a shock. But there's no-one else for me Debs, you know that."

He was right. I didn't see this coming. I played for time.

"I'm flattered and I'm honoured but what's the rush Adi? Let's just finish our degrees and we can talk about it then?"

He looked crestfallen.

"I haven't been completely honest with you. The thing is….the thing **is**…."

He hesitated over the words. Suddenly, incomprehensibly choked.

"My mum's been diagnosed with inoperable pancreatic cancer. We don't know how long she's got. I know what it would mean to her to welcome you formally into our family while there's still time.

I didn't tell you, but mum was pregnant before she had me, with a daughter she named Prisha. Prisha was stillborn. Mum's told me she sees you as the daughter she might have had. I know she would love for you to be a part of our little family. It's not Mum who's asking. She doesn't know I'm doing this. It's Dad who asked me to think about it."

He looked at the floor.

I reached for his hand.

"Adi, I'm so sorry about your mother. I can't tell you how much. Can you give me a little time to think this through?"

He nodded silently, lost in his thoughts.

◆ ◆ ◆

I thought of little else in the days that followed.

The thought of being with Adi, living with him was wonderful. The idea of committing to him for the longer term wasn't really all that scary.

But how did marriage fit in with this whole 'authenticity' thing? I'd only just got my head around my new journey, only just got started on my path. I hadn't authored this as an idea. And actually, neither had Adi.

How could he of all people ask this of me? Was he just like Wilson, raising my expectations, convincing me of the possibility of redemption then letting me fall?

No. Not Adi. How could he say no to such a request? And how could I?

I had no idea what to do. I needed to consult.

◆ ◆ ◆

Dammit. Leike had a big bag of ten pences and was hogging the phone on the landing.

"Mama! Hoe gaat het met jou?"

She was in for the long haul.

Reluctantly, I stuck my head round the door of the phone box at the end of our street. There were suspicious-looking puddles on the floor and it stank of piss. Shimmying around the edges of the box to avoid the puddles, I picked up the receiver. It reeked of stale cigarettes.

Caz answered the phone herself this time.

"**Caz!** How are you?"

She laughed her throaty laugh.

"Oh you know. The us-ual. Sad, lonely and single."

"What happened to that fireman you were seeing?"

"Ugh. Got on my nerves. Story of my life. So what's with you

Babes?"

"You won't believe this. Adi's proposed."

"Oh **my**. That's come right out of the blue. And pray tell me, just what's so tough about shackling yourself to that great sexy lump of a man?"

"Aww...come on. We're so young Caz. And besides, what seems to be driving the timing of it is Adi's mum. She's terminally ill."

"Aw. Shit. All but impossible to refuse then?"

"Seems that way."

"But really, Debs let's look at this objectively. Would you have ever thought about marrying Adi anyway?"

"Yeah. I suppose. Maybe one day. Just not now."

"So it's a timing thing?"

"Well yeah. Sort of. I guess."

"And how bad would you feel if you later married without Nyra being there?"

"Pretty damn shit I suppose."

"So there's your answer."

"Goddamit Caz. I was counting on you tell me to "Just say no!""

"Sounds to me Debs like it is actually something you want. Don't dismiss it out of hand."

"But a **wedding** Caz. You know what Mam's like. And how would we even pay for it?"

"Oh that's easy. Have a festival wedding."

"Never heard of it."

"Aww...it's just what it sounds like. A really relaxed affair. You have it in a field or a garden. Bung up a couple of tents or a gazebo in case it rains. Pile the food on trestle tables, keep it all very casual. No top table, no wondering who to put beside who, no speeches unless you want them. As simple as you would want. That's more you guys isn't it?"

"Yeah. I suppose that sounds just about do-able."

"You'll want a bridesmaid though?"

"Hahaha....you offering?"

❖ ❖ ❖

I told Mam that Adi and I were to marry.

"Ah. So you're pregnant then?"

"No, actually I'm not."

"Right. You'll be wanting Bill's replacement Ernie to do the ceremony? Not that you'll have met him of course. Being that you don't go to church anymore."

"No Mam. You know Adi and I are atheists."

Mam rolled her eyes and pursed her lips.

"**Atheists**. Ugh. Aren't they just people who're too lazy to be religious?"

Something snapped.

Years of pent up rage burst forth, tearing a cavernous hole in a carefully protected dam.

"**Soooooo**.....Mam! Why don't you tell me precisely what it is you do in the service of your precious religion?

You don't go to church. **You** don't pray. I bet you've never even **read** the Bible.

You **hypocrite**! You act like I've disappointed **you**? What about how much **you've** disappointed me? You've never hugged any of us. You've never told us you love us or are proud of us. You remember when I was ten and I asked you where I was before I was in your tummy? What did you do Mam? What did you **do**?"

Mam's eyes blazed. She raised her chin and said nothing.

"You did what you always do Mam. You snorted, rolled your eyes and walked away. It wasn't just any old stupid question. I was wrestling with something really important. I asked Da but he doesn't know the answers. **You're** the smart one Mam. You're the one who might have helped.

But you held back. You gave nothing. That's not how a mother's supposed to be. With you, it's just all bitterness, negativity, judgement and hate. It's not like we asked to be born. We didn't sign up for any of this. Why did you even **bother** to have kids? No wonder Davey is the way he is!"

I saw her jaw twitch at that last accusation.

I stopped, conscious that here I was lecturing my mother on how she should be.

What was the point anyway? I was exhausted. I was emotionally spent.

Mam finally responded.

"Have you **quite** finished Mrs. Simpson?"

"Why? Why do you call me that?"

"After Wallis Simpson. Everything was fine till she came along."

◆ ◆ ◆

Adi and I married on a fine day in July.

We'd discharged the legal side the day before with a brief ceremony in Eastwood Registry Office. Our witnesses were Caz, Adi's cousin Sal and Adi's parents.

Our wedding celebrations took place the following day in the leafy communal gardens of Adi's parents' building. They had erected a small marquee in case of rain, but the day dawned calm and golden.

Caz had accompanied me to a shop called 'Yesterday Once More' at the Barrowlands where I'd chosen a vintage 1930's bridal gown. An antique gold guipure lace Empire line, it had a surprisingly intact lining of double face silk charmeuse and – best of all – it cost just £35. It smelled slightly fusty, but Caz had hung the gown in their living room for a few days and it was soon infused with the scent of Maureen's jasmine joss sticks.

I topped the gown with a deep halo of flowers from Nyra's private section of the garden - intense blue delphiniums, soft pink Peruvian lilies, orange gerbera daisies and a cloud of babies' breath. Caz, as bridesmaid, wore a 60's satin maxi dress in a vivid wannabee Pucci print with a slightly smaller version of my floral circlet. Nigel, her last minute plus one, wore black chinos, an open necked shirt and the ubiquitous Stocks.

Adi smashed the Bollywood hero look in a cream silk salwar kameez, a circlet of flowers on his beautiful head. Best Woman Sal wore a black silk salwar kameez with a bright buttonhole of garden flowers. Her black hair had been swept into a soft chignon and she was wearing the most subtle make up. She looked gorgeous.

Nyra beamed in a fuchsia silk, gold braided sari, Clive on her arm in a cream linen suit with an open collared shirt.

Roddy's plus one was an elegant, quietly spoken boy called George. Roddy and George had taken Da to MacGregor and MacDuff and kitted him out with a full Jacobean kilt outfit with a matching plaid and brooch. Da had wanted the full version with the heavy wool Argyle jacket, but the boys convinced him he'd roast in the July heat. Roddy and George wore the same Dress Gordon tartan as Da, minus the plaid, that honour being reserved for the proud Father of the Bride.

Even Mam had made an effort. Da had taken her to Goldbergs and bought her a softly sprigged black and yellow midi dress with puffed sleeves and matching yellow pumps.

When Mam and Da entered the garden, a jangling, rustling Nyra rushed up to greet them with tears and hugs. Mam accepted the hugs without fuss and we all breathed a sigh of relief.

The tension between Mam and I was palpable. After the Wallisgate fiasco, even peacemaker Roddy hadn't attempted to negotiate a settlement.

Since the legal wedding had already been completed, Adi and I had agreed on a ceremonial Celtic hand-fasting ceremony in the garden. Beneath a flower-laden trellis arch we stretched out our arms and our humanist celebrant Sue wound two lengths of ribbon – cream silk and Dress Gordon tartan – around our joined limbs. We made our vows to one another and on Sue's instruction, drew our arms back to allow the ribbons to fall into a lover's knot.

Clive read a moving piece from the Lebanese poet Kahlil Gibran:

Love is a temporary madness; it erupts like volcanoes and then subsides. And when it subsides you have to make a decision. You have to work out whether your roots have so entwined together that it is inconceivable that you should ever part. Because this is what love is.

Love is not breathlessness, it is not excitement, it is not the promulga-

tion of eternal passion. That is just being in love, which any fool can do. Love itself is what is left over when being in love has burned away, and this is both an art and a fortunate accident. Those that truly love have roots that grow towards each other underground, and when all the pretty blossoms have fallen from their branches, they find that they are one tree and not two."

When he'd finished the piece, Clive looked to Nyra and smiled.

Ceremony over, amidst a flurry of rose petals, one of the first to congratulate us was Estelle. Prim as always in a neat mint green Jacques Vert suit with matching saucer hat, she rolled her eyes toward Nyra and Clive's home as she hugged me.

She giggled. "I see you **passed**!"

I giggled with her.

"But seriously Debsy, that man of yours....wow. Tot-al keeper!"

One by one our guests passed down the line, hugging us and offering us their best wishes for our future together.

When it came to Mam's turn, I braced myself.

Mam placed her hand on my shoulder and, nodding, said:

"You've done well Deborah. You've done well."

Line up over, Nyra summoned some helpers and brought out the food. She had outdone herself. Brightly covered trestle tables groaned beneath a fragrant smorgasbord of home-cooked dishes and delicacies from Nyra's homeland – Alo Gobi, Aubergine Pratel, Bombay Potato, Chilli Paneer, Egg Plant Vathakal, Mathi Aloo, Mutter Paneer, Okra Baji, Pumpkin Curry and Soya Pratel. Dishes of various Dahls and Sambars lined up beside colourful containers of rice – Pulungal, Ghee, Lemon, Tamarind and plain Basmati.

For dessert Nyra served up Kesari – a delicate semolina halva with roasted cashew nuts and raisins; Kithul Payasam – a creamy tapioca pudding flavoured with palm kithul syrup and ginger; Semiya Payasam – a creamy vermicelli pudding with coconut milk and nuts; plus a tropical fruit salad with kulfi – an Indian ice-cream made from sweetened condensed milk, cream, saffron and vanilla.

As we ate, Caz's brother Nigel strummed soft acoustic classical guitar pieces. He'd improved greatly since I last heard him bashing out discordant riffs in their family home. Her arm around my shoulder, Caz inclined her head toward her brother:

"Nige was gutted when he found out you were to be married. He's always had this thing about you."

I was speechless.

"Whaaaat Babes? You mean you never knew?"

As the sun dipped behind the tenement buildings, Mhairead appeared at my side and lent me a soft pink cashmere wrap for my bare shoulders. She looked beautiful – all golden curled and rosy cheeked. She'd flown down from Shetland with her partner Rob. Rob had inherited a successful plant nursery from his father and Mhairead had taken over the business paperwork.

"That was such a beautiful ceremony Debs. Rob and I are planning to marry very soon because....well...."

She cupped her hand beneath her tummy.

"We're expecting Debs. And we've something really important to ask you."

She looked at Rob and he took her hand.

"We would love for you to be the baby's godmother."

"Right. Wow. That's such an honour. Thank you very much. But I'm really sorry - I can't accept it."

Mhairead looked shocked. She looked at Rob. This was clearly not what they'd anticipated.

"It's just that I'm an atheist Mhairead. I don't believe in God. So I wouldn't be a good choice for you at all."

"What does that matter Debs? It's not like Rob and I believe."

"I'm so sorry. I just can't. It would be hypocritical. It wouldn't be right."

Mhairead drew back as if slapped. Too late. To avoid making a hypocrite of myself, I'd inadvertently accused them both.

"Why are you being so **difficult** Debs? So selfish. You're my best friend. I thought you'd want to do this for me? You didn't even want me to be your bridesmaid."

Mhairead burst into tears and headed toward the bathroom, closely followed by Rob.

Adi appeared at my side, a concerned look on his face.
"What's going on puchki?"
I sighed.
"Don't worry about it Ads. We can talk about it later."

It's not that I had imagined authoring your own beliefs would be easy. But I thought it would be achievable with diligence and conscious effort. I hadn't reckoned on the degree to which the journeys of others would impact and derail.

It just wasn't that simple.

◆ ◆ ◆

Adi and I delayed our honeymoon to spend as much time with Nyra as we could.

Her oncologist Dr. Harris told us that Nyra's cancer had already spread into her stomach, spleen and large bowel. Though inoperable, he recommended chemotherapy to slow the growth.

"How long do we have doctor?" asked Clive.

"Hard to say with any accuracy. But not long."

"Are there any promising drug trials Nyra could participate in?"

"Yes, there are one or two you would qualify for Nyra. I can look into that for you if you like? You would have to stay in hospital for the duration of the trial though. So the results can be carefully monitored."

"No." said Nyra "If my time has indeed come, I will die at home."

Dr. Harris continued.

"We can book you in for your first cycle of chemotherapy from this coming Monday if you would like that?"

Nyra smiled.

"No. No chemo. I know what it does to the body and I would like to depart this world with as much dignity as can be managed."

"We could prolong your life by anything up to six months Nyra" said Dr. Harris.

Adi's eyes brimmed.

"Mum, please. We're not ready for this yet. Please at least try."

Nyra looked at the floor. After a few moments, she nodded.

Nyra booked her first cycle of chemo at the Oncology Day Unit at Hairmyres Hospital. But before the first session, she asked me if I could please sit with her for her donation cut:

"You're a woman Debs. You have such beautiful hair yourself. You'll understand what this means."

"I don't understand Nyra."

"Rather than wait to lose my hair and have it go to waste, I'm donating it now so it can be made into wigs for other women with cancer."

Ho boy.

Tina, a specialist volunteer hair stylist, came to carry out the cut. From her bag she removed a ruler, some ponytail holders, scissors and a large, resealable plastic bag. I held Nyra's hand while Tina combed out the glossy, ebony tresses. I was amazed at just how long Nyra's hair was and what little grey it contained.

I asked Tina about the ruler. She winced apologetically.

"Sorry. I have to measure the lengths. If they're less than ten inches they can't be used."

Tina tied Nyra's hair into about a dozen mini ponytails. When the scissor blades snapped together on the first cut, Nyra raised her chin and a small tear appeared in the corner of her eye.

Each ponytail was cut about six inches from Nyra's scalp and another ponytail holder wound on the end to hold the hair section together. Eventually when all the ponytails were cut and the ends bound, the whole lot was bundled into one braid and placed in the resealable bag.

Tina styled what was left of Nyra's hair into a short bob. She would lose the rest of it in time, but at least this softened the blow for now.

In the days that followed Nyra's first chemo cycle she was unable to eat without throwing up. Adi and Clive coaxed her to try small portions of plain food like mashed potato.

"It tastes of nothing." said Nyra. "This isn't food. Food is for pleasure. I'd rather not."

She developed painful mouth ulcers and took to sucking on little ice lollies to alleviate the discomfort.

After the first cycle of chemo Nyra had a CT scan to check whether the cancer had continued to spread. It had.

Dr. Harris suggested a break of a month then a second round of chemo.

"No. Enough already." said Nyra.

Nyra's remaining months were filled with as much care and love as we could give. As her body grew weaker, her smiles increased. The nurses from the palliative care team treated her with the utmost tenderness and respect. She rewarded them with gratitude and laughter.

As I sat with her one day, I asked her how it was she remained so cheerful in the face of death.

"It's not death I'm facing daughter. My soul will be freed from the tethers of this decaying body. Death is not something to fear. It's how we are released from the cares of the material world and samsara - the endless cycle of birth and re-birth. As we gradually rid ourselves of the illusion that is the material world, we realise the true nature of reality and become one with Brahman, the supreme being. My time has come and I am ready."

As the end drew near, Nyra would sleep for longer and longer periods.

Adi would read softly to her – some of the many hundreds of verses from the Bhagavad Gita and some her favourite verses of Kahlil Gibran's poetry. One in particular brought a lump to my throat:

You would know the secret of death
But how shall you find it unless you seek it in the heart of life?
The owl whose night-bound eyes are blind unto the day cannot
Unveil the mystery of light.
If you would indeed behold the spirit of death, open your heart
Wide unto the body of life.
For life and death are one, even as the river and the sea are one.

Adi and Clive moved Nyra's bed closer to the window so she could watch the changing colours of her garden. Delphiniums and lilies faded gradually, making way for sunflowers and dahlias.

The leaves on the Japanese acer put on a vibrant show of red, yellow and orange. As the evenings grew shorter, the air more chilled and the breeze carried away what was left of the Acer's leaves, so too did Nyra leave us.

In the end, it wasn't the cancer that took her. She developed a blood clot in one of her veins which then caused a pulmonary embolism. She died quietly in her sleep, surrounded by those who loved her.

I had so many questions. Would Nyra have lived her life differently if she'd believed we have but one life? If she'd believed that there was no divine plan, that life is meaningless and simply a collection of random occurrences?

I didn't know. But what I did know was that Nyra had been happy. And Nyra had given and received nothing but love.

I asked Adi why he thought that religion for some was a source of peace and lifelong happiness and yet for others a source of suspicion, resentment and seemingly endless conflict.

"Well...." He said "It's something I've thought about a great deal and it strikes me that at the heart of it is the distinction between 'belief-in' and 'belief-that'. You can't simply reduce one to the other."

"I don't get it."

"If I said to you that for some religion takes the form of what I call 'worship of the dead letter' it might make more sense. That is to say that for many, religion seems to be a non-engaged activity, the rigid following of a set of laid-down activities, rules and even attitudes toward people or things without any genuine understanding of or concern for why things in that tribe or community are the way they are. I see that as 'belief that'.

Genuine belief-in or faith seems fundamentally different. It doesn't seem to arise from the cognitive side of human nature, from consideration of what is provably true or false, or what is stated in a holy or a history book. 'Facts' don't touch belief-in. You can't reason your way to faith. Not that it's un-reasonable as such. It's just that reasoning is not how you get there".

I thought of my own unsuccessful attempts to gain faith.

"So how **do** people get there?"

"Well...I think sometimes people have a fundamental hunger for a sense of order that would deliver them from the existential discomfort of experiencing life as simply one event after another. Think of how often you hear people say 'That was meant to be' or 'Everything happens for a reason'.

Those aren't statements of logic, for there are no facts which would support them. They are statements of hope, statements of faith that there is something more than randomness in the universe. If someone is predisposed to that kind of hope – and I think more people are than not – they're most likely to attach it to the set of rules or prescriptions they've naturally grown up with, being perhaps Catholic or Protestant, Hindu or Jewish.

If you think about it Debs, people all over the world almost inevitably believe that the religious - or at least religious-seeming - structure they are born into is the only 'true' one.

Because these beliefs don't originate in a series of rational propositions which lead to a reasoned conclusion, when people argue over conflicting belief systems it seems no resolution can ever be found, for these are not arguments of logic. Challenges to the beliefs will be responded to emotionally and it is the overwhelming power of that emotion that has driven pretty much all of the worst of human conflicts.

Sadly, I think for many who attach that driver of hope to a set of – particularly religious-seeming beliefs – this can be done without actual belief that there is, for example, a God. It almost doesn't matter. In that sense, you could say it is simply a focus for tribal bonding."

"So hardly worth dying for then?"

"Absolutely. Although there do seem to be people for whom the belief-in is much more fundamental. It comes almost from a deep involuntary conviction, something that is perhaps instilled in them at a stage before they develop sufficient critical thinking skills to reject it.

I think that's what my mum had. That's why there was no conflict within her. I didn't get that, because it wasn't instilled in me from an early age. Nor was I steered toward belief-that. I don't know why. But fortunately I don't have an issue with randomness in life. It excites me if I'm honest."

"Adi – this might be a daft question. But is atheism a 'faith'?"

He looked thoughtful.

"If you mean the belief that 'there is not' in terms of a god or deity, well in some ways yes, I **guess** so. For you can't really prove or disprove it."

◆ ◆ ◆

Nyra was cremated following a moving ceremony at Linn Crematorium.

We who mourned her wore white to symbolise Nyra's purification, her release from the material world.

Atop her casket was a radiant photo of Nyra, the frame draped in a garland of flowers. As each mourner arrived, we inclined our heads toward the casket, saying not 'Rest in Peace' - for her soul's goal was not to rest - but Om Shanti, expressing the wish that Nyra's soul be liberated from the cycle of life and death.

We scattered most of Nyra's ashes in her favourite spot on the banks of Loch Lomond, retaining a small amount in a jewelled container for a very special purpose.

CHAPTER 12 - COMING HOME

Before she left us, Nyra had gifted Adi some money and asked him if he would consider a honeymoon in India, most particularly so that she might have some of her ashes scattered in her homeland.

Adi asked me how I'd feel about that.

"Well, yes, of course. I've never been abroad but if I were to choose a destination, I can't think of a more interesting one than India. And if we can do this for your mum too, then yes. Absolutely."

"I've been thinking" said Adi, winking "if we go to Goa we'll be obliged to make endless rounds of the rellies. That's not really anyone's idea of a honeymoon. How about we visit the neighbouring state of Kerala instead? It's where Mum and Dad met after all."

So Kerala it was.

Often described as 'God's Own Country' Kerala is sandwiched between the dramatic rise of the Western Ghat mountains and the glittering beauty of the Arabian sea.

I was instantly captivated by this verdant paradise of lush, green, scenic landscapes and crystal clear beaches. The backwaters a magical maze of lagoons, criss-crossed with rivers, canals and shallow pools.

Adi had arranged for Harjit, a hollow-cheeked local man, to be our tour guide and drive us around our various destinations. Harjit collected us at Trivandrum airport in a slightly battered white Mahindra Xylo. Harjit explained that having a driver was common in the more rural parts of India, as the roads are generally in a deplorable condition and road rules – such as they are – are not exactly followed.

"Self-driving in India.." – laughed Harjit "is most dangerous to the mental and physical vell being!"

From the airport, we drove for several hours on crude roads pockmarked with gaping pot holes. If there were indeed traffic rules, I couldn't fathom what they might be. Dusty cars, rusty lop-sided buses, ancient taxis, bunting-bedecked trucks and the ubiquitous, beetly little tuk tuks all zigzagged haphazardly from one side of the road to the other, drivers honking, beeping and gesticulating. But, bizarrely, always smiling. We passed entire families balanced precariously on groaning 50cc motorcycles and a bony youth on a rickety bicycle with a live, protesting sheep tied around his shoulders.

It was insane. Utterly terrifying, but exhilarating.

When we reach Cochin, our first destination, Harjit dropped us at the entrance to our hotel, unloaded our luggage and drove off. I asked Adi if he were planning to stay at a different hotel.

"Hmm. Unlikely. An allowance is given to drivers for accommodation, but most often they'll sleep in the car to save the money."

Next morning a smiling Harjit arrived bright and early to take us on our tour of the sights. As we drove to our first stop-off, Harjit chattered amiably, animating his speech with the charming head wobble that's so prevalent in Southern India. He boasted with enormous pride that Kerala has the highest level of literacy in the whole of India, with over 90% of both males and females having fairly advanced skills in reading and writing. Harjit himself read three newspapers per day – two national and one local.

We first visited the Paradesi Synagogue. Built in 1568 it's the oldest active synagogue in India, built by Portuguese speaking Jews. From the tall ceilings of the main hall, vast glass chandeliers glittered in the light from the large, open windows. Hand painted, blue willow tiles from Canton adorned floor and ceiling, each tile different from every other in its design. A grand pulpit with ornate brass rails took centre place and an intricately carved teak Ark housed the four silver and gold-cased books of the Torah.

We then visited Mattancherry Palace, more commonly known as the Dutch Palace. This was used by the rulers of Cochin as their Royal house. The central courtyard houses a temple of the royal deity Pazhayannur Bhagavathi and there are two other temples on either side of the palace dedicated to Lord Krishna and Lord Shiva. Harjit pointed out the flooring, which looked like black marble but was created with a mixture of burnt coconut shells, lime, plant juices and egg whites. In the days to come we would be repeatedly astonished by what Keralan enterprise could make out of the humble coconut.

After a lunch of black chana and coconut stew, we dropped into a group tour of a tea estate and a spice plantation, the tour guide carefully explaining all aspects of the horticulture and what happened to the products after harvesting.

As we drove from one tourist sight to another, Harjit entertained us with an endless stream of stories, facts, statistics and history. He proved to be immensely knowledgeable and I asked Adi why someone so highly educated would be driving a taxi.

"Sadly, there aren't the same opportunities here as we would have."

At the Heritage Museum, Harjit walked us round the various exhibits, explaining in painstaking detail each exhibit's place in Kerala's history and culture. At some points I would have preferred to wander off on my own, but Harjit was proudly demonstrating his almost encyclopaedic knowledge and it would have been inconceivable for us to allow our attention to wander.

In time Harjit lead us to a tall display cabinet lit up from many sides. In the cabinet was just one item – a small rock.

Harjit said:

"And this.....**this** is the God Shiva come to earth in the form of a rock."

He scanned our faces for a reaction. I must have raised an eyebrow or twitched.

Harjit laughed.

"We're not crazy people you know. We don't literally think this rock is God. It's symbolic. It symbolises for us that God is in all the things – in the trees, in the mountains, in animals and in people. Everything it is connected. Everything it is divine."

En route to our next hotel, I asked Harjit why hoardings advertising Indian products – Kingfisher beer, Thums Up cola and Parachute Hair Oil – most often featured fairly overweight men and women.

Harjit grinned and wobbled his head:

"It is being a sign of wealth and status in India to be carrying veight."

On the morning of day four we drove to Allepey and joined a crew of three for an overnight cruise on a traditional Keralan Kettuvallam. First built in around 3,000 B.C. these armadillo-shaped rattan-covered houseboats were once used for the transportation of rice, spices and other goods and now mainly carried visitors to and from the many wildlife sanctuaries and nature reserves.

The hull of our boat was formed from long wooden planks bound together with coir rope and coconut fibres coated with a resin made from boiled cashew nut shells.

As the crew manoeuvred the boat using long bamboo poles, we wound our way silently on the palm-fringed backwaters, gliding slowly through numerous lagoons, lakes, canals and rivers.

Although of fairly rough traditional construction, the boat's interior had finely carved wooden furnishings and a clean, modern, bathroom and kitchen. The small bedroom was dominated by one large bed, a mosquito net covering most of the sleeping area.

In addition to the Captain who steered the boat, an on-board tour guide pointed out local flora and wildlife while a local chef prepared gourmet Keralan cuisine for us.

When, with full stomachs, we retired to bed, Adi drew me to him and began to remove my cotton sundress.

"Adi, no. The crew will hear."

"Debs, people in India don't have the luxury of the privacy we enjoy. If people were shy about lovemaking there would be no children."

In the morning, we awoke to the sound of the crew preparing breakfast. As the sun rose over the tranquil, liquid gold waters of Vembanad lake, landing geese skimmed the lake's surface and touched down with an audible plop.

Local people emerged from rough wooden cabins on the lake's edge. Women in vivid saris, their hair loose and long, stepped into the water to make their morning ablutions. I was captivated by their beauty and it struck me how wonderful it must be to live so simply in such a paradise. I said as much to Adi. He smiled and ruffled my hair.

"Ah Debs. Did you not once accuse me of romanticising the poverty you lived in?"

And indeed I had.

Backlit by the rising sun, we stood on the bow of the boat and scattered Nyra's ashes on the surface of the lake. Adi read from the Hindu Holy Scripture, the Bhagavad Gita:

"The Spirit is neither born, nor does it die at any time. It does not come into being or cease to exist. It is unborn, eternal, permanent and primeval.

The Spirit is not destroyed when the body is destroyed. It is eternal, all-pervading, changeless and immovable. It is beyond space and time.

Death is certain to one who is born....thou shalt not grieve for what is unavoidable."

"Goodbye Mum" said Adi "Whatever lies beyond, know that you have been loved."

◆ ◆ ◆

For breakfast, the boat crew served puttu, a delicious cylindrical steamed rice cake which they had cooked in a mould with grated coconut. It was served with fried ripe bananas and coconut milk and a little shot glass of toddy, the local fermented palm wine.

Harjit was there to collect us on our return and as we drove to our next destination, we talked endlessly about many aspects of Indian culture, philosophy and religion.

I began to notice how much easier it felt to express myself – no, **be** myself when immersed in such a foreign culture. I had no real understanding of the rules or expectations so I felt free from my usual practice of making what I thought were the right allowances, tip toe-ing around certain delicate concepts and making assumptions about other peoples' mind sets or status. I felt strangely liberated.

I could not know and did not need to know where Harjit fitted into the strictures of his social group and culture. Harjit – had he even been interested – had no way of slotting me into what would define me in my own culture – class, religion, politics.

We were freed in the moment to simply stand in one another's light.

It struck me that if I were to find myself in some genuinely meaningful way, to author my own beliefs and values, I would feel much freer to do this if removed myself physically from the strictures and expectations of my own tribe.

CHAPTER 13 - TROUBLE AT T'MILL

After our wedding, Adi and I rented a small one bedroom flat in a red sandstone tenement just off Byres Road, just until I finished my degree and we could plan our future together in greater detail.

Adi had secured a two-year contract as a Programme and Logistics Assistant with the International Red Cross, based in both the U.K. and in Lebanon.

In harrowing phone calls and letters home, Adi poured out his despair at the daily death and destruction he witnessed in his organisation's efforts to alleviate the suffering of the legions of homeless and displaced.

The initial establishment of the state of Israel, he explained, had displaced a hundred thousand Palestinians into Lebanon which had not only shifted the previous religious balance in favour of Islam - sparking a long and bloody civil war - but consigned generations of Palestinian families to a life of squalor, statelessness and insecurity.

The Palestinian Liberation Organisation had established a quasi-state in Southern Lebanon using that as a base for revenge raids on targets in North Israel. Israel responded with damaging attacks not only on PLO bases but also civilian buildings, including hospitals. Thousands of Lebanese and Palestinians were killed by Israeli bombardment, the vast majority of them civilians.

Adi was in no doubt where the blame lay.

"They used illegal **cluster** bombs Debs."

"Who did?"

"Israel of course. They were given those bombs by the U.S. on the explicit understanding they were to be used strictly for defence.

I see it every single day. They treat the Palestinians like they're less than human. They've been thrown out of their lands, they have no homeland, no security, no state, rights or status. The camps are dangerously overcrowded. They lack basic infrastructure or sanitation and the refugees can go months without either electricity or safe water. Do you know how humiliating these conditions are for a once proud people?"

"Aww...come on Adi. The Israelis are defending themselves against attack. What else can they do? Where else should they have gone after the bloodbath that was the Holocaust? Where might they have felt safe? Israel is their homeland. It always has been."

"Says **who**? It's not like the land was empty. They had to go in and take it, ejecting others who had done nothing wrong and in turn now have no homes, no lands, no income and nowhere to go."

I didn't want to hear it. I stuck steadfastly to my conviction that, given their history, if any group could show the rest of us how to be, it would be the plucky Jews.

"You're being **anti-Semitic** Adi."

"Take that **back.** Immediately. You're doing what I told you it was dangerous to do. You're confusing religion with power politics, with all the destructive emotional baggage that entails. You said yourself that a large proportion of Israeli citizens are atheists. So no religious issue there, yeah?"

This isn't about being Jewish Debs. A large number of Jews – in fact a large number of Israelis – are horrified by what their leaders are doing in their name. This is solely about what territorial disputes throughout history have been always been about – that is, protecting a piece of land and its resources.

Name a land that hasn't at some time been fought over in the same way? The difference here is that public sympathy is predominantly on the side of Israel, for obvious reasons. No-one cares about the Palestinians for their existence was largely unremarked upon before now. And **Deborah**..."

Adi only called me Deborah when he was angry.

"Tell me Deborah, just why is it that you hold the Israeli nation to a much higher standard of behaviour than every other nation throughout history?"

It was a rhetorical question. Adi knew perfectly well that the plucky Jews had my heart. Ergo, I was not open to reason.

In the end, we argued about the situation in Lebanon so much that we were forced to agree to disagree. I was at all times predisposed to support Israel, Adi the Palestinians.

◆ ◆ ◆

In July 1983, a year after Adi, I graduated.

Following a long, drawn out ceremony in the Great Hall, chattering graduates, family members and flocks of lecturers and professors in colourful robes, ermines and mortarboards filed out into the Quadrangle for a congratulatory reception.

Standing alone and dejected by the table of sherry and canapes, Mam and Da looked entirely miserable. So far removed from the identity and reassurances of their tribe, Mam and Da were lost. No amount of alcohol seemed sufficient to dull the pain of their imagined exclusion. I don't know why I put them through that. I should have known better.

In the after-graduation 'milk round', I was hired as a Research Writer with an independent documentary film company called Time for Change. At first the job was mostly desk research, but within a few months I had the opportunity to accompany the film crews on some, if not all, of the location shoots.

The stories we covered were many and varied: the growing movement for same sex couple adoption; the Romany diaspora in Europe; teenagers breaking free from the Amish in Pennsylvania; the growing anti-vax movement in the U.S.; honour killings and acid attacks in India; and ethnic tensions in the Middle East.

When given a brief to research a future programme to be entitled 'The State of Things' exploring the prospects for youngsters growing up on U.K. council estates, I read no further than the title and asked for an appointment with Simon, our Programme Director.

"Sooo…" asked Simon "to what do I owe the honour?"

"This programme on the youngsters on council estates, Simon. It worries me. I mean… there have been **so** many programmes already about how they're doomed to life on the dark side, lacking ambition, leading this shadowy existence on welfare benefits and crime. So I was wondering if there was any way we could maybe include at least some of the success stories to come out of the estates… you know, the talented musicians, actors, scientists, politicians, bankers, civil servants… to maybe give the thing a bit of balance at least?"

Simon smiled.

"Debs, have you heard of a guy called Ralph Glasser? Grew up in the most extreme poverty in the Gorbals, tutored himself and won a scholarship to Oxford in the 1930's? Now an eminent economist and psychologist? That's the kind of story we want to focus on."

He winked.

"If you'd actually read your brief, Debs, you'd know that. So go find the rest of the success stories. These are the stories that need to be told."

When it aired, the programme was controversial. The public had grown accustomed to the lie that prospects for council estate children were irredeemably dire. When the challenge was thrown out that it didn't have to be that way, not everyone responded positively. A substantial and hugely vocal majority of council estate residents and their bullish representatives were incensed. The local angry tabloid – while unable to dispute the success stories we'd highlighted – resented the implication that there could be more. Success stories did not sell newspapers – well, at least not that one.

Researching a programme on the tens of thousands of orphaned children in Israeli-occupied Gaza, I was appalled by the desperate conditions in which these children lived. Years of conflict had stolen their childhoods and burdened them with not only unimaginable grief, but a complete absence of any hope for the future.

I thought again about what Adi had experienced and reported back to me. I regretted my automatic taking of sides. As with most disputes, it just wasn't that simple.

◆ ◆ ◆

I thought a lot about Mrs. Graham's and Gran's stories and resolved to put together a report of my own by interviewing more women of their generation who'd grown up in similar circumstances. My plan was to put together an anthology of voices or perhaps suggest it to Simon as a potential future documentary.

It was easy to find the women. So many had departed the squalor of the slums to be given houses on the new council estates. There they'd remained and – given the fortuitous change in their housing conditions – why would they not?

Again and again I heard the same stories of women who'd barely made it into their teens becoming pregnant with child after child; losing some of those children; struggling through each and every day, week, month and year with one goal - just to survive. And as their girls reached puberty, so often they too became pregnant and the whole cycle of misery continued. I heard stories of immense personal sacrifice, hopelessness and despair. If the grim, sepia locations were sometimes different, the stories were depressingly and similarly sordid. As time went on, I found myself asking just one question. Why? Why did they do it?

I know you'll say they hadn't the choices we have now. There was no contraception. But that's not the question I'm asking. The question I'm asking is what is the **purpose** of it? All of it. Any of it?

I realised I couldn't do it. Didn't want to do it. I didn't ever want kids. I couldn't see the point of an infinite regress and progress of self-sacrifice, lives laid on the altar time and again to serve the greater good of I knew not what.

I would have to broach this with Adi.

◆ ◆ ◆

Adi was, as always, relieved to leave behind the desperate conditions of the refugee camp and have some much needed time out.

On his first night home we had a nostalgic meal at the Chowdhury Club. Adi was in great spirits. He didn't want to talk about what he'd left behind, so we talked about my work, our families, our friends and our hopes for the future.

He was considering applying for a permanent post in Queensland, aiding displaced and dispossessed aboriginal peoples.

"You could join me there, yeah Debs? I mean, you could work from anywhere?"

I smiled. It sounded lovely actually. And there was less for us to argue about, the rights and wrongs in that particular situation being so far beyond dispute.

But there was something we needed to discuss.

Our lovemaking that night had a poignant urgency to it. As Adi slept, I lay awake and considered the implications of what I was about to do. It might be that Adi felt the same and I was worrying for no reason. I didn't think so.

You might say that this was something we should have discussed before we'd even considered marriage. But you'll remember the circumstances. There wasn't time.

The morning dawned crisp and autumnal. I made Adi idli as I always did on his return.

Adi noticed that I was quiet during breakfast.

"What's bothering you puchki?"

"Adi. Do you want children?"

He smiled.

"Of course I do. I'd like a boy . . . and a girl. A girl with your beautiful eyes. And maybe one of them would have the chess gene. They say it skips a generation. How happy would that make Dad...?"

He stopped and scanned my face.
"Speak to me Debs."
"I don't want children Ads."
He laughed.
I glared.
"Sorry Debs. It was just the shock. I don't understand. Why would you not want children?"
"Wrong question Adi. The question for me is - why would I **want** children?"
"Because it's human nature Debs. We're hard-wired to procreate and pass on our genes. If we didn't, there's every chance we'd regret it in later life. When it's too late."
"I don't **believe** this Adi. You're the one who told me that, as intelligent beings governed by logic, we could and should rise above our nature, our basic instincts. I mean....that's **exactly** what you said. Isn't it?"
"Yeah, but think about it. We could give a little someone the chance to enjoy an existence they wouldn't otherwise have. We could give and receive unconditional love ... create and mould a brand new life. What could be better?"
"Can you **hear** yourself Adi? Remind me of that favourite line of Rand's you're always quoting?"
Adi looked at the floor and said softly:
"I swear by my life and my love of it that I will never live for the sake of another man, nor ask another man to live for mine."
"Can't you see Adi, how selfish and immoral it would be to produce a consciousness without its consent? You simply presume that experiencing life is a privilege no consciousness would refuse. Why do you believe that? All this 'life is a gift' is just so much **bullshit.**
What if the child were unhappy? What if we realised we'd only created a child to give **our** lives meaning? So we could run from our own fears, avoid finding meaning for ourselves? We can't simply pass on the torch without having run the race. And from what I hear from the women I've interviewed and having a ringside seat for all the years of Mam's unrelenting bitterness, to have kids you

have to give up almost all of yourself.

And yes, I know just how selfish that sounds, but wanting to . . . wanting to . . . **control** and derive satisfaction from someone else's life, isn't **that** the ultimate selfish act? Forcing life onto another human being should be the hardest decision you ever make. Yeah, I didn't choose to be alive but now that I'm here . . . after all that Mam has given up . . . this life is **mine**. I have an obligation to make it count. You as much as said so Adi."

"Debs....if everyone thought like you, there wouldn't **be** a human race."

"Sorry Ads. I just can't bring myself to care about that. I don't want to perpetuate my genes, my tribe, the whole myopic world view, the hate, the suspicion, the conflict . . . all of it. People glibly say 'but children make the world a better place'. No they don't. They grow up to be adults. And look what adults do. And so many people are so unhappy and unfulfilled. You said so yourself. I can't be responsible for that."

He came over to my side of the table and took my hand.

"Debs. Don't be scared. You won't **be** like your mother. How many people do you hear say that having a child is the best thing they've ever done? This is your chance to right the wrongs Debs. How do you **feel** when you look at a newborn baby?"

"That's just it. I feel nothing. Ads, how can you of all people ask me to do that which can never be undone on the hearsay of people who cannot but say what they may not mean?"

Adi sighed.

"Sorry Debs. You've lost me."

"Think about it Ads. What parent would dare to say they regret having had a child? Society demands we say it's the greatest thing because to say otherwise is unthinkable. No-one would ever say it. Therefore, who could possibly base such a crucial decision on the opinions of those who cannot say otherwise?"

Adi did make many more attempts to win me over. But by the time he was due to return to Lebanon, we both knew there was no future for us.

◆ ◆ ◆

I knew I would have to tell Mam and Da that Adi and I were no longer together.

I put it off for as long as I could. I could hear Mam's response:

"Typical Mrs. Simpson. It's always been all about **you**. Always too selfish. After all we've been through to bring you up."

I took a deep breath.

"Mam. Da. Adi and I have split up."

"Oh" said Mam.

"But why hen?" said Da. You've always been really good the gither."

"I don't want kids. Adi does."

I searched Mam's face. She gave nothing away. She stood, walked slowly across the room and sat next to me. She put her arms around me, she closed her eyes and she held me.

She didn't squeeze tight. She didn't say anything. She just held me for a long time.

And she never called me Mrs. Simpson again.

EPILOGUE

Adi took the job in Queensland.
On the day he left he wrenched my heart from my chest, packed it in his rucksack and waved goodbye. He had said he could do without kids. He had said he just wanted to be with me. But I couldn't do that to him. I couldn't do that to us. The time would inevitably come when it would tear us apart.

Drowning in waves of fear and emotional turmoil, I felt at times I couldn't face another day. I cannot lie. There were times when I weakened. When I told myself I could do this for him, just to feel him close to me once more. But to do that...to do **that** I'd have to commit to doing that which could never be undone.

At times the pain was so intense as to be almost pleasurable. And in that space I found myself sharply, immediately and exquisitely alive.

As I write this, know that I take a knife through my heart, peel back the layers and show you my innermost self. You may judge, but that's okay. I invited you in after all.

My recurring dream of thwarted island-reaching has gradually receded and a new dream has taken its place. I am alone on an island. The air is heavy with the scent of exotic flora and the deep hum of cicadas. I am aware of a presence. That presence is neither good nor bad, just a sense of something that is there and is in the process of revealing itself. It is not in a hurry. I am not in a hurry. It will come when it will come and it will be what it will be.

Lately I find myself inhabiting that space at will and in my waking hours. The silence is warm and enveloping, the atmosphere laden with possibilities. And in the deep stillness of the moment,

I sense that I am not alone. You may say – if you are predisposed to think that – that in this moment I am connected with God. I would say – because I'm predisposed to think in a different way – that I have found myself.

◆ ◆ ◆

I kept on the lease for our flat and continued working with Time for Change. My job has taken me to furthest flung places and while – in the hurly burly of flights, filming schedules and research - I no longer seek that elusive sense of belonging, I generally find something of value, something thought-provoking and life-affirming in each country I visit, in every community I reach out to. Perhaps one day I'll settle in one of those countries, but for now I'm calm, focussed, centred and satisfied.

Caz joined a small, independent touring theatre company. Maureen and I went to see her in a production of Pygmalion at the Citizen's Theatre in the Gorbals. We clapped till our hands tingled, eyes brimming as we exchanged looks of familial pride. In Will, a fellow cast member from New Zealand, Caz has finally found a man who inspires rather than irritates her. They're planning to move in together.

Roddy and George live quietly with their greyhound Marcus in a rented cottage in Callander, a small town in Perthshire. George writes code for a start-up gaming company in Edinburgh and Roddy contributes to anthologies of short stories and poetry. To help with the bills, Roddy writes short features for the Reader's Digest. There, he seems to be building quite the following. His recent article entitled "Do not Seek the Truth" created controversy by claiming that there is no such thing as The Truth – that is, that all 'truth' is relative and subjective. Seems obvious to me, but it would appear from readers' reactions that many people find that notion entirely offensive.

Roddy and George grow more fruit, vegetables and herbs in their garden than they can consume and barter the rest at the local farmers' market for much of what else they need.

And they make the most delicately delicious elderflower wine. One evening when George had gone to bed early and Roddy and I were draining the last few glasses from of one of the demijohns, Roddy asked me:

"Debs. Do you ever regret what we did to Davey?"

"**Huh?** I don't understand. What did we ever do to Davey?"

"We didn't let him in."

◆ ◆ ◆

Sal and Nigel are in love. With each other that is. They'd bonded at our wedding over a shared passion for the music of Jefferson Starship. Sal smiles a lot these days and not everything she wears is black.

Estelle has just been declared 'Newcomer of the Year' by Franchise Life magazine. She dinked her Mini Cooper and found the whole experience of the auto repair shop so grubby and distasteful that she borrowed some money from her parents and set up Pink Auto Spa.

P.A.S. is basically a relaxing, interior designed lounge with soft music, coffee and snacks. Patrons can have their nails done, browse magazines and use the internet while they wait for service, M.O.T. or quotes. The repair shop is entirely hidden from sight and service add-ons include designer upholstery scenting and glitter paint. The original P.A.S. has been so successful that Estelle has sold ten franchises nationwide, with five more in the pipeline.

Mhairead had a little girl – Diane Louise. I've written to her several times and sent gifts for her daughter. She has yet to reply.

Clive has rejoined the international chess competition circuit after a long absence. He complains that many of his opponents have scarcely outgrown their nappies.

Due to emigration to England, the U.S., Canada and New Zealand, together with an increase of secularism and intermarrying, the Jewish community in Scotland has declined steadily. In 1988, its circulation terminally low, the Sentinel closed its doors. Rumour has it that it was Moshe's refusal to print what the community wanted him to print which hastened the Sentinel's demise.

Mam and Da are much the same. I guess it's much too late for any dramatic change. If Mam is relieved she won't be having grandchildren, she hasn't said so. And she's said nothing about Roddy and George. I sometimes wish she could open her heart to us as I have opened mine to you. But I expect it's so mummified by layer upon layer of scar tissue as to be bereft of all tenderness. And Da? Da endures. That's all I can say.

Uncle Boaby has been charged with several counts of kiddy fiddling. It's always appalled me that a judicious choice of wording can make such a heinous crime sound like a jolly pastime. Roddy wasn't surprised.

"Aww…come **on** Debs. The guy was weird. All the kids thought so."

"Didn't see it myself."

Roddy laughed.

That's because you're……ready….one, two, three….

"**Naïve!**"

From time to time I would ponder the fates of those others I'd crossed paths with on my journey so far – Miss Campbell, Mrs. Barr, Pippy, Bridie, Bill, Rachel, Wilson, Norrie, Mima, Linda, Irene, Erik, Mr. Garry, Moshe, Natan, Ellen, Leo, Tony Caprioli, Lucy, Greta, Frida, Leike, Veerle, Fong, Sying, Eddy, Mags and Harjit.

Little did I know that in 2004 Mark Zuckerberg would launch a social network platform which would allow us all to meet again.

Oy Vey!

◆ ◆ ◆

And finally, you'll want to know about Adi. We've kept in touch of course. Adi loves Australia and he's been busy setting up a marketing co-op to help Aboriginal village artists sell their Dreamtime paintings. He's in a relationship with a co-worker called Amber. He is happy. Adi deserves to be happy.

ABOUT THE AUTHOR

June Russell Laing

Edinburgh-based June Russell Laing is the author of recently released novel 'Finding Fealty' and a similarly themed excerpt from a novelette entitled 'Crossing the Line' which was published in an anthology of alternative women's fiction.

A first-class Honours graduate in both Philosophy and Comparative Religion, June is a recipient of the Holtz Prize for Logic and the Caird Prize for Moral Philosophy. June has taught Critical Thinking skills to students undertaking university entrance exams.

When she's not constructing arguments, June swaps her thinking cap for a hard hat, designing and building one-off homes with her husband Andrew Laing, several of which have featured in interior design magazines.

More of a Domestic Luddite than a Domestic Goddess, June loves to travel and to paint. She and husband Andrew overwinter in sunny South Africa where June runs art classes for beginners and samples cheap and plentiful South African wines.

June's favourite novels are those which weave challenging philosophical and religious questions into stories of everyday lives and everyday people, thus making potentially inaccessible academic ideas both comprehensible and – hopefully – more relevant.

BOOK CLUB DISCUSSION QUESTIONS

What do you think of Mam's statement that a Protestant marrying a Catholic is 'like a dog mating with a cat?'

Why is Jesus largely portrayed in Western society as pale skinned and blue eyed?

What was the difference between what Miss Campbell wanted for Debs and what Debs wanted for herself?

Why did Debs say her tribe did not – strictly speaking – have religion?

In what way was the 'religion' that Wilson offered different from that offered by Debs' tribe?

How did Mrs. Graham's final poem make you feel?

Why did Debs reject the idea of sex with Wilson?

Why was Debs so in thrall to the 'plucky Jews'?

Why did Debs reject her 'Catholic hating' history?

Why did Mam achieve a level of accommodation with Roddy and Davey but not Debs?

Why did Davey turn out so different to Debs and Roddy? Was he inherently bad? Or was he – as his social worker Brenda suggested – a victim of a demonised underclass?

Was Lucy's devotion to the Communist ideal in some sense 'religious'?

Was Jesus' teaching in any sense communist?

How do you feel about the idea of a 'Chinese' Jesus or an 'African' Jesus?

Given Nyra's devotion to her religion, why did she draw back from initiating Adi into the Hindu traditions?

If Nyra's religion made her happy, would it matter if the caste system were merely 'the tool of a repressive political regime'?

Why do you think it is that most religious people 'choose' the religion of the social grouping into which they are born?

Why would Adi have seemed 'like a bushman' to Debs' family?

Is it wrong for a newspaper to cater to the bias of its customers?

Can and should people make individual, rational and conscientious choices about what they believe? Are there any circumstances in which it's okay to simply accept the philosophical and moral system handed down by your social group?

Do you think humans really do avoid addressing their own existential freedom?

Was Adi's idea of a sort of 'matrix' of people with overlapping beliefs a realistic one?

What do you think of Mam's idea that atheists are people who are too lazy to be religious?
Do you agree with Mhairead that Debs was being selfish when she refused to be a godmother? Would it have mattered if she'd just

gone along with it?

Do you think Nyra would have lived her life differently if she'd believed we have but one life?

What do you think of Adi's distinction between 'belief that' and 'belief in'?

What do you think of Debs' belief that it's immoral to create a consciousness without its permission?

Is Debs right that people might have children to give their own lives meaning or to run from their own fears and avoid finding meaning for themselves?

Do we have a responsibility to perpetuate the human race?

Do you believe that parents would say they regret having a child? And if they wouldn't, what is the significance of that?

When Debs told Mam she didn't want children, why did Mam go to her and hold her?

When Roddy said of Davey that he and Debs 'didn't let him in' what did he mean? And how significant might that have been?

Printed in Great Britain
by Amazon